MURDER ON THANKSGIVING

VICTORIA MATTSEN CRIME SERIES

BOOK 8

IFEANYI ESIMAI

eISBN: 978-1-63589-808-8
Print ISBN: 978-1-63589-809-5
Audio ISBN: 978-1-63589-810-1
Cover design by coveredbymelinda.com

Published by ShotReads, an imprint of
Ciparum LLC
270 Sparta Ave., Suite 104, PMB 152
Sparta, NJ 07871

Get a FREE copy of The Rookie!
Join my Newsletter for updates, giveaways, teasers, and a FREE copy of the prequel - The Rookie. Click here or scan the QR code.

ACKNOWLEDGMENTS

My heartfelt gratitude goes out to my family and friends, whose unwavering faith in me fueled this project from the very start.

I also want to extend a special thanks to a group of incredible individuals whose generous spirit has made an indelible impact on this project, and for that, I am forever grateful.

Erik S
Nneka Anaebonam
Craig Martelle
Jenn Davidson
Chinwe Anyamele
Obioha Emezie
Renee
Okechukwu Obua
Romeo Richards
Ikenna Emeghara
Charles Onunkwo
Adaeze

Every one of you has helped shape this journey in your own unique way, and I couldn't be more thankful. Your support has not only made these books a reality but has also inspired me as I continue to tell Detective Vikki Mattsen's story.

To all the readers, thank you for inviting Detective Vikki

Mattsen into your lives. It's been a joy to share this adventure with you.

Here's to the stories yet to be told.

PROLOGUE

Marriage was a comfort but also a torment. The woman's smiling face filled the crosshairs of his scope, and his finger tightened on the trigger. The image in his scope, with some imagining, looked like the tattoo on his wrist—a skull caught within crosshairs. That was one connection he hadn't made in a long time.

He pushed the toothpick in his mouth from one side to the other and eased off on the trigger. Another opportunity was mere seconds or minutes away. One shot, one kill. He smelled victory. The outcome was a foregone conclusion.

He had all night if he wanted it that way. This was not the Middle East or Eastern Europe, where escape could sometimes be an issue.

Sometimes he liked his job, and other times he didn't. In a way, it was like his marriage. Nobody had told him what the after-the-fact looked like. Nor let him in on the secret that two becoming one was as difficult to understand as God the father, the son, and the holy spirit being three persons in one.

He'd learned on the job, especially about the enemy within. Maybe he would have been better off never picking up a sniper's rifle or putting a ring on it. Becoming a sniper and getting married had both taken their toll on him.

Movement in the window he was watching pulled him away from his thoughts. Satisfactory execution meant he needed to know what the elements were doing—the winds especially.

His eyes drifted to the two buildings on each side of his target's home. The lights were off. They were unoccupied like the one he was in. The fireplace was asleep, and the owners were gone for Thanksgiving.

The room he'd picked was a little boy's. He had a Pikachu poster on the wall and a bookshelf with the *Diary of a Wimpy Kid* series.

He focused on the chimney of the building he was watching. It was wide awake. A mixture of black, gray, and nearly white smoke spewed from it and glided in the inky-black, cloudless sky like Dementors as if New Jersey had gone Rowling.

Should he have reconnoitered the property and gotten a little closer to figure out what glass the window was made of? Too late now, and dangerous, too. At least he had a bullet that penetrated most surfaces.

To be doubly sure, he'd wait until his query got as close to the window as possible.

Maybe he would have had a second sniper with instant follow-up shots like in the field. But this was no field assignment. This was him getting extra credit on his own.

In his scope, the woman's face once more filled the crosshairs. He shut his left eye and took a deep breath. He let it out slowly and pulled the trigger.

"*Veni, vidi, vici,*—I came, I saw, I conquered."

CHAPTER ONE

Vikki lay on the couch—knees bent, head resting on Ted's thigh in his apartment, feeling melancholic. She was dressed in a warm cream sweater and blue jeans. She was well protected from the cold. It'd been twelve years since that fateful day when Vikki had joined the police academy after Alexis and her dad had been murdered in cold blood. Seven, since Bruce had died in the line of duty. She wasn't there yet to forgive herself.

She sipped her prized coffee, Americano, with French vanilla syrup. It hit the right taste buds. Bitter, sweet, sour, and everything in between—precisely how she felt. She took Ted's hand and placed it on her chest.

A documentary about the Pilgrims and their interaction with indigenous people worldwide and the birth of Thanksgiving was on TV. The deep, rich voice of the presenter penetrated the thoughts going on in her head.

Ted ran a finger along her temple. "You look worried. Everything okay?"

Vikki didn't answer right away. She sat up and put her

coffee on the table. "When things are going my way, I always look for ways to screw it up."

"That's not true. Everyone has a lot of good days and one bad day thrown in. Talking can help."

Vikki inhaled and let it out with a sigh. "Today is my friend Alexis Devoe's father's birthday. Thanksgiving is always a reminder. After she and her father were killed, my mind was set on finding and...murdering who'd slaughtered them. Then Levin convinced me to join the police. Two wrongs don't make a right. I probably would have been dead or been imprisoned for multiple life sentences for murder."

"Okay, do you want to talk about it?" Ted said, his hand moving down to her arms. He massaged and kneaded her muscles.

Vikki let out a satisfied moan.

"I'd just come back from France, where I went to college. It was St. Patrick's Day. I walked into the house and met Alexis and Uncle Mike. He was the uncle I never had. He was happy to see me. We exchanged pleasantries. Then he went back to join his guests. Later that night, I went out with friends. Alexis went to a bar. When I returned to the house later that night, police were everywhere. At first, they wouldn't let me into the house until one of the cops recognized me as the girl in one of the family pictures. I vowed I was going to get revenge."

Ted took a deep breath and let it out slowly. "You've helped other people navigate their pain. It's now your turn to help yourself."

Her phone rang, interrupting the conversation. It was now routine. The caller was her chief, Levin. Moments later, Ted's phone rang. It only meant homicide.

CHAPTER TWO

Vikki drove up the windy road to number thirty-four Poole Road in her dependable Ford Explorer. Light shined through the windows of some of the homes she passed, with smoke curling out of their chimneys. Others only had the security lights on—nobody was home.

Each house was on at least three to four acres of green lawn, undulating or flat, peppered with golden leaves. The neighborhood, she imagined, would be scenic during the day.

Most of the other trees had shed their leaves apart from the evergreens. The bare branches under the glare of an unusually bright moon looked like overturned trees with their roots in the air.

After Thanksgiving, most homes would have Christmas trees and lights on display. When snow blanketed the lawns by December, the whole of Poole Road would be postcard perfect.

Vikki couldn't help herself. She lowered her window and sniffed the air, hoping someone was burning wood in their fireplace. The odor and cold air reminded her of happier times in her childhood. Alexis, Santa, Christmas, and lots of presents, until they'd been taken from her.

Strobe lights loomed in the distance, and Vikki's countenance faded from good to bad. The crisp air she'd enjoyed moments ago lost its luster. She closed her window and focused on her destination and its surroundings.

Vikki parked on the road, hung her shield on a lanyard around her neck, and got out of the car. The wind tore at her. She shivered, understanding the family's violation with the interruption of their pre-Thanksgiving preparation. She turned up the collar of her peacoat and walked up to the front door.

Two police cruisers, the CSU van, and Gomez's car parked in front of a three-car garage. An ambulance with its engine running straddled the grass and the tar.

A flash of light in the hedge close to the building caught Vikki's eye. It was a uniform. She saw another by the lawn. *What are they searching for?*

Vikki smiled at the uniform standing in front of the yellow police tape. She signed the logbook, and he handed her one CSO—crime scene overall and booties for her shoes. Vikki sighed. Stepping into the CSO was easy, but she hated the prospect of sometimes hopping on one leg as she tried to slip the bootie over her shoes—necessary evil. You don't want to contaminate the scene.

"Emm...you-you can hold onto my shoulder," the uniform said.

"Thank you." Vikki did, and a minute later, she walked in.

It was a large foyer with a staircase leading upstairs. To her left was a sitting room, one of several. And to her right was the crime scene.

"Mattsen, good to see you," Gomez said.

Gomez was in his overalls. Vikki knew that underneath it

he was dressed in a black suit, white shirt, and no tie, like Marlon Brando in *The Godfather*.

"I was beginning to wonder if they somehow missed informing you. I'll bring you up to speed. CSU investigators are still combing the crime scene. The ME hasn't arrived yet, so we don't get to investigate until both CSI and ME are done." Gomez's voice was now almost a whisper.

Vikki took in the scene. Three men in white overalls combed the scene. Vikki could tell that one of them was Dennis Mallory from his round-framed glasses. He ran the CSU for SIPD. A meticulous fellow, he often showed up at crime scenes even when he had capable investigators to handle the job.

Gomez propelled her toward the sitting room on her left. "The victim is thirty-two-year-old Mary Beecham. She lived in Los Angeles and came to spend Thanksgiving with her parents, accompanied by her daughter and husband. The rest of the family is in the living room on the other side of the foyer. EMS gave the men something to calm them down."

Vikki frowned. "Why?"

"Losing your daughter and wife after dinner is not exactly a happy event."

Vikki raised her hands, palms out. "Okay, I get it. What happened?"

"They were in the dining room after dinner, talking when it happened."

Vikki was surprised Mrs. Beecham didn't live in New Jersey. She'd save her questions for when Gomez finished. But Gomez had stopped talking and stared at the wall. Vikki followed his gaze to a framed picture of a woman in a wedding dress.

"Is that the victim?" Vikki asked.

Gomez nodded. His Adam's apple bobbed up and down. "I just thought of Nia. What is this world coming to?"

Nia, Gomez's twenty-six-year-old daughter, lived in California. Vikki could only imagine what was going through his mind. "Don't worry, Nia is fine." She didn't know that, but she had to offer some platitude, just like the girl's parents hadn't expected what had happened to their daughter. Right in their home, just before Thanksgiving. "How old is their daughter?"

Gomez chewed his lip. "The grandmother said five years old."

"They finished dinner. What happened next?"

Gomez sniffed—stroked his chin. "Yes, they'd finished dinner, and Mary Beecham was talking about something funny they'd seen at the airport. She stopped in mid-sentence and collapsed to the floor." He shook his head. "They thought it was part of the act. But her father said he heard a crack, then his daughter fell."

"Jesus," Vikki said. "It must have been awful."

"That's an understatement. The husband rushed to her side. Her eyes were wide open, he said, staring. Then he noticed blood in her hair and called nine-one-one."

Vikki didn't ask if she was alive after the gunshot. The ambulance would be racing to the hospital by now. They were still around to treat any cases of emotional breakdown or shock in the victims.

The front door opened, and the ME and two investigators stepped in, dressed in CSOs.

CHAPTER THREE

Vikki acknowledged the ME with a nod. She tried to smile but couldn't conjure it. Less than an hour ago, they'd been talking about death. Then this had come in.

"Dr. Brandon, always a pleasure to see you," Gomez said. He nodded to the ME's assistant, who pushed a gurney.

"The feeling is mutual," Dr. Brandon said.

Gomez stepped closer, lowered his head, and said, "Can I talk to you for a second?"

Dr. Brandon raised an eyebrow and took in the crime scene. He gestured to his technician to carry on. "I'll be with you in a second."

Vikki cocked her head, her interest piqued. She feigned interest in a framed photo on the wall.

"We'll be honored if you and Victoria can join us for Thanksgiving dinner," Gomez whispered.

Dr. Brandon opened his mouth to say something, but Vikki beat him to it.

"Mike!" Her voice was a loud whisper. "I've been standing here with you for the past twenty minutes, and you didn't think you should've mentioned it to me?"

Gomez sighed. "It's a guy thing. I'm old-school." He glanced around with an "I just realized we have a job to do" expression. "Let's talk about it later."

Ted nodded and excused himself. "Dodged a bullet there," he muttered and went to join his team.

Vikki almost forgot where she was and was about to launch into what chauvinistic pigs men were when he saw the little girl with blonde pigtails wearing a jumper and holding a doll.

Vikki walked over to her and stooped low. "Hello, I'm Victoria. What's your name?"

The girl looked at her, tilted her head to one side. "Are you a policewoman?"

Vikki laughed. "Yes."

The girl laid her doll on the floor. "This is Barbie. She's sleeping like Mommy. But she'll soon wake up."

Vikki's heart broke. A lump formed in her throat and wouldn't go away no matter how many times she swallowed.

Vikki raised her head to the sound of approaching footsteps. A woman with gray hair, dressed in a cream sweater and white khaki pants, walked up to them. Her eyes were red. The remnants of her eyeshadow dark smudges around her eyes.

"Mary, I told you to stay in your room," the woman said in a quivering voice. "You're bothering the lady." She attempted to smile, but it didn't turn out great.

"It's okay," Vikki said. "I'm Detective Victoria Mattsen." She was about to extend her hand for a handshake and held herself back. "I'm so sorry for your loss."

"S-Susan Cooper. T-thank you. It's..." The woman paused.

Vickie knew she was about to give the automatic response: *It's all right*. But it wasn't okay. She'd lost a daughter.

The woman's eyes were red. "Come on, Mary, let's go.

Bring Barbie with you." She turned to Vikki. "I'll be back. The men are a mess. I guess it hasn't hit me yet."

"Bye," the little girl said and left with her grandma.

Vikki watched them walk away. The desire to find whoever stole the child's mother away from her was overwhelming. Vikki wanted to tear the place apart in search of clues. Scene contamination was real, and being too hasty could jeopardize things. She promised herself that whoever did this must be brought to justice.

Vikki went back to Gomez. He stood by the window staring into the yard, following the flashlight of the uniform searching the lawn.

"A penny for your thoughts?" she asked.

Gomez sighed. "I'm lost for words. Thanksgiving is days away. People are busy getting ready to celebrate with family and friends, not commit murder...I would think." He let out a breath. "But here we are. We have to come back tomorrow to interview the husband and father. I couldn't get much from them."

Vikki nodded.

"If this were in the inner city, I'd say it was a drive-by." He paused and thought for a moment. "No, not a drive-by. Maybe a kid visiting from somewhere found—or someone found—a rifle and pulled the trigger, not knowing it was loaded. And the bullet ended up here."

"It's possible," Vikki said. "But we know there are no coincidences. We have our work cut out for us." She turned to the sound of footsteps. It was Mary Beecham's mother.

"Detective Mattsen." The woman's voice was low and quiet. "I know you have questions. My husband and Greg... Mary's husband...are out of it." A mixture of a laugh and a cry escaped her lips. A tear rolled down her cheek. "I'm trying to be strong for my granddaughter."

Vikki walked over, hesitated, then peeled off a glove and squeezed her shoulder. "We can do this some other time."

She closed her eyes and shook her head. "If I talk about it, the sooner the nightmare will be over."

They sat on the sofa. Mrs. Cooper walked her through the events. They'd arrived from California the day before. She was excited to see her granddaughter after two years. They'd finished dinner, and Mary had been talking.

"I got up to get dessert, apple pie, from the kitchen island where I'd left it to cool," Mrs. Cooper said. "Mary offered to get it. And I said no, carry on with the story." She pulled a tissue from the box beside her and dabbed her eyes. "I should have been a bad host for once and let her. That bullet wouldn't have found her." She sobbed.

Another person that believed it was a random bullet, thought Vikki. She gave her a few moments to compose herself. "Mrs. Cooper, I'm going to ask some difficult questions, but it's only part of my job."

She nodded. "Call me Susan."

"Susan, Mary and her husband, did they appear worried? Like something was bothering them?"

Susan shook her head. "They seemed happy. I've been married for a long time. A couple can show you only what they want you to see. I don't think they had any issues."

Vikki pursed her lips. "Is there anyone you think might have wanted to hurt Mary?"

Susan raised her hands and dropped them on her lap. "Nobody I can think of. We brought Mary up to respect people. She's a people person."

Vikki closed her notebook. She'd brought it out more for effect than to write much. The more she'd been at this job, the more salient points from an interview remained in her head. She mostly wrote down numbers. "Thank you, Susan, that's all. Is there anyone we can call for you?" She gave her a card.

"No."

"If you remember anything or want to talk, feel free to call me."

Gomez walked over when Susan had left. "Mallory has something to share."

CHAPTER FOUR

Dennis Mallory stepped out of the dining area. He pulled off his mask, followed by his gloves. He threw his head back and inhaled deeply.

Vikki watched his ritual and waited. Before being tapped to head CSU, Dennis Mallory had been a homicide detective and brought that hawk eye into investigating crime scenes.

"You can come this way," Mallory said. "The ME is on the other side. The bullet came through the glass and struck the victim." He pointed at a hole in the glass window. "When the ME is done, we'll check for exit wounds. We've looked at that display cabinet right there, and at the walls, too. We found nothing."

"You think it's still in the body?" Vikki asked.

"Most likely." Mallory nodded toward the window. "I see you already have uniforms combing the grounds."

"Footprints, cigarette butt, shell casing—just in case," Gomez said.

Vikki walked closer to the window. It was at least six to seven feet above the ground. Somebody standing outside would have a difficult time seeing into the room. Unless the victim were by the window, which she wasn't, it would be nearly impossible to get a shot in.

"I doubt you'll find any casings," Mallory said. "The bullet came from...I'll say at the same level as where it struck the victim. Or from a higher position, but from a distance."

Vikki gazed through the window. It was all bare trees. With their leaves gone, she saw a couple of houses far ahead. Could the bullet have come from that distance? "Like from this general direction."

Mallory gave a subtle nod. Then he switched gears and went into what Vikki called professor mode.

"Retrieving the bullet will be a major plus to the investigation. Knowing the type will be crucial in identifying where the shooter got his bullet, then maybe who, by elimination." Mallory paused and made eye contact with each of them to make sure they were still with him.

Vikki was captivated. Sometimes she saw the TV show *How It's Made*. It blew her mind the processes a simple product went through to become what it was in the store.

"This was no gangbanger drive-by shooting. The bullet went through the glass like it was designed to and still hit its mark."

"You're saying it wasn't a lucky shot?" Gomez said. "A special bullet."

"A regular off-the-rack bullet might drop to the floor after penetrating the glass. Or leave cracks on the window and not do major damage." Mallory pointed at the window. "This was like poking a hole in a balloon with a needle. We checked for shards of glass, but there were none."

Vikki exhaled. "In other words, she was assassinated?"

"Barring further investigation—maybe. What I know for sure is that a highly sophisticated rifle and bullet were used."

"Was the shooter on the premises?" Gomez asked.

Mallory frowned. "Let's step outside, and I'll show you."

He headed for the door, stripping off the rest of his protective overall and bootie.

Vikki and Gomez removed theirs too and put them in an evidence bag.

The cold bit into Vikki once more. It felt worse since coming from a warm place.

Mallory walked down the stairs, cut across the shell of a flower bush, and stood under the window. "I'm at least six feet three inches tall. I can't even see into the house. Shooting someone from here is out of the question."

Vikki looked in the general direction the window faced. "The houses are far away. Could a bullet travel that far and still do damage? That supports a high-powered rifle theory. Or, the perp was in the adjoining woods?"

Mallory nodded. "The woods would be my best bet. But the homes shouldn't be ruled out."

"I'll have some uniforms check out the woods," Vikki said. "Call on the houses and see who has CCTV or Ring doorbells."

"We might be lucky," Gomez said. "My neighbor has a camera pointing into the backyard of his home. He's seen deer, bears, foxes, and even a mountain lion."

Mallory chuckled. "There are no mountain lions in New Jersey. It must have been a Bobcat. They resemble each other, but the lion has a longer tail."

Gomez shrugged. "I saw the video. It could have been a snipped lion."

"Snipped mountain lion?" Mallory tossed his head back and roared with laughter.

Vikki hoped none of the uniforms outside the house saw him. It was uncharacteristic of him. He was always serious.

Mallory wiped his eyes with the back of his hand. "Anyway, we're more interested in a person with a rifle. The scene is all yours once the ME is done. I'll get my people, and we'll be out of here."

Before returning to the house, Vikki called one of the uniforms to check. He asked him to knock on the houses all the way to the beginning of the street and ask about suspicious characters and video cameras. "I guess some people are on vacation, please list empty homes so we can call on them after the holidays."

Vikki put on fresh shoe covers and went back into the house. She found Ted, focused, taking pictures. He was working fast. The double shutter sound of the camera filling the silence.

Gomez leaned closer to Vikki. "He said he's almost done."

They waited until Ted and his assistant had gone through their process, documenting evidence around the victim. Only when they were ready to carry the victim away did they approach. Vikki got her first close view of the victim. She saw her daughter's face in her.

"There's no exit wound," Ted said. "This was a kill shot. The bullet is probably still in her head."

Gomez chuckled. "Where else could it be?"

"I've seen a case where the bullet ricocheted inside the cranium and came down the neck and into the lungs without exiting the body."

Gomez's eyes widened. "No way."

Vikki sighed. "Guys." She turned to Ted. "Time of death, if you don't mind."

"Sometime around eight," Gomez said. "That's what her mother said. She'd checked the time before tragedy struck."

Ted nodded. "Once we get her back to the lab and retrieve the bullet, if it's intact, ballistics testing will provide a lot of answers or generate new questions, which should help."

Ted and his tech crossed their checklist. Satisfied they'd covered everything on it, they placed her in the bag. The tech zipped the bag up and secured it with the belts on the gurney. He pushed a lever, and the stretcher sprang up. He pushed it toward the door.

Vikki followed Ted outside. "What's the plan for later on?"

Ted removed his overalls and peeled off his gloves. "The chief wants the autopsy done as soon as possible."

Disappointed, Vikki said, "Got it. That means you'll be spending the night in the lab. I'll drive back to my place, then. Tomorrow will be a busy day for me, too."

"Okay," Ted said. "I'll see you when I see you."

CHAPTER FIVE

Vikki walked down the Beechams' long, dark driveway to her car. Her hand hung by her side, not too far from her Glock. The woods were bare, but that talk of what people with back-yard cameras had captured was on her mind.

Once in her car, she cranked up the heat. She'd been surprised there were no onlookers. It only confirmed to her that Thanksgiving preparation was in full swing. She hoped the police officer canvasing the neighborhood returned with something useful.

From the discussions with Mallory at the crime scene, she'd treat this as an assassination until proven otherwise. Had Greg Beecham made himself unavailable because he didn't want to implicate himself when his emotions were still raw?

If Vikki wasn't driving, she would've searched the police database to learn more about the Beechams. The closest thing to researching on her own was a phone call away. She reached for her phone on the dash and called her friend, Angie Baxter.

Vikki was surprised Angie was vacationing instead of

working on a story. She'd perfected the art of sticking her nose into one thing or the other. An investigative journalist, she wrote for *The Chronicle*, a local St. Ives Newspaper. Sometimes, Vikki picked her brain for research on cases she was working on and vice versa. They tried to respect each other's professional turf.

Angie had traveled to Georgia to visit family for Thanksgiving. She and Vikki had a cooling-off period after Halloween. Angie suggested the real perp for the recent vampire murders was free. She'd made a good case that had Vikki rattled. She was trying her hand at fictionalizing the event into a novel. After a frosty few days, Vikki had forgiven her.

"Victoria Mattsen, I'm on vacation. Why are you bothering me?"

"Good to hear from you, too," Vikki said.

"How can I help you?"

Angie had grown up in St. Ives and knew a few more people and their backstories than Vikki. Vikki exhaled. "What can you tell me about the Beechams?"

"The Beechams? I don't know any Beechams?"

"Sorry, the Coopers," Vikki said.

"Mary Cooper?"

"Yes."

"Nothing, really," Angie said. "They're normal folks. They do not have a tunnel under their home to the graveyard. Her mother is a homemaker, and her dad is a lawyer. Wait, are they fine? You'll tell me something that will spoil my vacation."

Vikki blew out air through her mouth. Angie was right. She shouldn't have called her. "Don't worry about it. Enjoy your vacation."

"Don't you dare hang up! The genie's out of the bottle. You might as well tell me because I'll go digging."

"All right, someone shot Mary Cooper in the head. She's dead."

"Oh no, oh no," Angie said. "Last I heard about her was when she moved to California." There was a pause. "I'm guessing Beecham is her married name?"

"Yes. She was visiting her parents with her husband and little girl."

"This is unbelievable. She was the sweetest person. There's no dirt there at all. Why are you worried about the case?"

"It seemed like an execution," Vikki said. "She was shot from afar."

"I know where they live. It's a quiet neighborhood. The possibility of a drive-by shooting is remote. Maybe someone pulled a trigger somewhere, and Mary was unlucky." Angie paused. "Terrible in so many ways. Anyway, I'll let you know if I dig up anything."

Vikki continued home. Every homicide she'd investigated in the past had been tragic, but this one felt personal. Was it the little girl? Having her mother snatched away in such a brutal fashion was heartbreaking. A new resolve to get to the bottom of it washed over her.

Vikki had lost her parents at a young age, too. She hoped the little girl's father had nothing to do with it, for her sake.

That night, the little girl was on Vikki's mind. She saw the parallels between their lives and felt an urge to revisit her past. By morning, Vikki had reached a decision.

CHAPTER SIX

Vikki arrived at the PD just before nine in the morning. She'd added a scarf to her outfit—khaki pants, a sweater, and her coat. On her way, she spied a free parking space at the coffee shop and drove in.

The barista smiled. "What can I get you?"

"Two large black coffees and two sausage, egg, and cheese croissant sandwiches." One for her and one for Gomez.

Only when she left the store and was driving away did it occur to her that since Thanksgiving was around the corner, a box of Joe for the squad wouldn't have been out of order.

The fact that they had no suspects or persons of interest in yesterday's murder was like a mosquito buzzing at her ear —constant and irritating.

She took the elevator and rode up to the first floor, carrying the coffee on a tray with the sandwiches in the middle. The smell was right under her nose and was driving her crazy. She passed Jody's table, but she wasn't there. She would catch up with her later.

The detective squad room with chairs and computer desks

seemed to be arranged without rhyme or rhythm. It had the feel of a call center. Most detectives who worked together sat side by side. She was no exception. Her desk was next to Gomez's.

Even though the holiday was coming, crime never went on vacation. Everyone was entitled to vacation time. To ensure there was always someone to handle leaves, someone was on call every day, and more could be called up if there was an emergency.

Vikki looked ahead to her desk, and Gomez wasn't there yet. She hoped he'd come soon. She didn't want the added duty of babysitting his coffee and sandwich.

"Victoria, good morning. How are you?" said a voice beside her.

"Hey, I'm doing great. What about—"

She'd turned to see who was greeting her and almost dropped the tray. She scanned around to make sure he was talking to her. She was the only one close by. He beamed at her.

"I'm...I'm fine," Vikki said and continued to her desk, glancing over her shoulder a few times. She couldn't believe that Sean McClane was talking to her. This was like something out of a bad dream.

Detective McClane had been a Field Training Officer when Vikki was a rookie. In her first week after graduating from the police academy, she'd met up with fellow new police officers at the Bull Dog Pub. On her way back from the bathroom, McLane had blocked her path, propositioned her, and proceeded to cup her bottom.

Vikki, an abuse survivor, had kneed him in the groin so hard he'd gone under the knife for an emergency orchiectomy. McClane had become the poster child for male jokes, and had tried to make Vikki's life miserable since then. Vikki had left that precinct and forgot all about McClane. She had been surprised to find him in St. Ives after she'd relocated from New York almost a decade later.

He'd picked up from where he'd stopped and continued to torment her with rude jokes. All of a sudden, from out of the blue, he was being nice.

Not wanting to be in the same space as McClane, Vikki dropped the food and coffee on her table and headed to the captain's office, hoping he was there. She knocked and stepped in.

Captain Levin sat behind his desk, dressed in his usual navy-blue suit, white shirt, and red tie. He had a piece of paper in his hands and glanced up when Vikki walked in.

"Mattsen." He cocked his head. "Everything all right?"

Vikki forced a smile. "Good morning, sir. Sorry to bother you. It's...it's McClane..."

"What about him?"

Vikki took a deep breath and let it out in a rush through her mouth. "Over the years, I've gotten used to him being mean and obnoxious. This morning he was smiling and asking me how I was doing. It's giving me the creeps."

The captain smiled. "About time. Do you know what carrying all that meanness does to a man's heart?"

Vikki shrugged. "A heart attack? He's still here. He's been carrying it well, I guess."

Captain Levin chuckled. "It seems like Sean is in a good place now. It took a while, but he's come around."

A moment later, Vikki said, "There's something else. I want to investigate the Devoe murders...on my own time."

"Mike and Alexis?" Captain Levin said, his eyebrows shooting up.

Vikki nodded.

The chief was quiet. He made a steeple with his hands. When he spoke, his voice was soft. "Victoria, it's been twelve years. Are you sure you want to do that? Sometimes it's better to let sleeping dogs lie."

Vikki swallowed. "Last night…last night a woman was murdered, and I saw her little girl. It brought back memories. It reminded me of promises I made that I haven't kept. I've let it lie for too long. It will be strictly on my own time."

"Of course. If that's what you want, you have my blessing." Levin smiled. "I still know some people in New York. I can make a few calls."

"Thank you, sir. But that will make it somewhat official. Let me do it all the way—on my own time."

Captain Levin pursed his lips and nodded slowly. "I understand." He raised both hands, palms out, and laughed. "No meddling."

Vikki let out a breath that was about to choke her. He'd seemed offended for a second.

"I'll take a few days in the New Year and see what I can find out."

"Sure. What about the shooting last night?"

Vikki told her what they knew, which was close to nothing. "Dr. Brandon planned to do the autopsy last night, and the bullet should be going for ballistic testing this morning. The husband and father of the victim were too grief-stricken to speak, so we'll return today to get their statements."

They both turned to a knock on the door.

Gomez walked in. "Good morning. I hope I'm not too late."

Captain Levin returned the greeting. "We were talking about yesterday's murder. Didn't we have a similar case about six weeks ago?"

Vikki drew a blank. She turned to Gomez. He appeared clueless too.

"I think that was the week we were investigating the professor."

Captain Levin nodded. "Okay, tell me about yesterday."

Gomez sat and added his two cents to the narrative. Mostly the same as Vikki's account.

"Hopefully, you'll get some answers today. And Mike, Mattsen is interested in a cold case in New York—"

Gomez glanced at Vikki. "New York?"

"Just giving you a heads-up," the chief said. "And she has my blessing...as long as it doesn't interfere with her work. Okay, keep me updated." He paused for a moment and cocked his head. "I feel like I'm missing something. Ah, the mayor's on vacation. No wonder he hasn't called about the murder."

CHAPTER SEVEN

Gomez shut the door quietly behind him. "Mattsen," he said in a hushed voice. "Are you serious you want to do this?"

Vikki knew he meant New York. "Do what?" She feigned ignorance.

"Unwrapping a breakfast burrito that is twelve years old? Nothing there would resemble what went in."

"Sometimes that's what a cold case needs to get solved—time." Vikki attempted a smile, but even her lips had their doubts. She took a moment to reflect. "It's like old wine. It mellows with age. People forget, drop their guards, or believe it's water under the bridge."

She continued toward their desks, and Gomez followed.

"If you put it that way, it makes sense," Gomez said. He took in a deep breath and exhaled. "Vikki, you're like a daughter to me. I don't want to see you dig up memories that will only hurt you."

Vikki knew he was right. But nobody seemed to understand what she was going through. It had been a long time. If she hadn't entered the police force and gone looking for the killer, or killers, after the murders, maybe she would have found them by now. Or serving two or three life sentences. The sound of Gomez's voice brought her out of her reverie.

"I want to believe Ashton PD gave it their best shot back then. You might step on toes that wouldn't appreciate something they'd already dealt with rearing its ugly head like shingles."

Vikki pulled out her seat and sat. The reasons Gomez gave had gone through her mind, too. She decided to change the subject. "Do you know who said hi to me this morning?"

Gomez smiled and eased into his chair behind his desk. "Who?"

Vikki glanced around conspiratorially and said, "Detective Sean McClane."

Gomez cocked his head. "No way."

"He did," Vikki said, feeding off the excitement in Gomez's voice. "I walked into the squad room, and he said hello. I walked as fast as I could to Levin's office."

"Wow. After all these years he's coming around. There must be a God."

Vikki shaking her head said, "I still don't trust him. I'm two hundred percent sure he's up to something."

Gomez grinned. "Here comes work."

Vikki turned. Maria Santiago came up to her. In her hand was a piece of paper.

Vikki smiled. "Hey."

"Good morning," Santiago said and extended the paper to Vikki. "The uniform who covered the scene last night said I should give you this. I saw him in the parking lot on his way out. He said it's a list of the homes he saw last night. The ones circled were empty. The homeowners we saw all said they didn't see anything out of the ordinary."

Vikki scanned the list. Four house addresses were circled. "Thank you so much. I appreciate it." She felt bad. She hadn't even asked for his name in the dark last night. She'd seen him around, though, and knew his face. "Do you know his name?"

"Officer Drake. John Drake. He and Acosta joined at the same time."

Vikki smiled. "Ah, how is Acosta?" She knew something was brewing between the two of them

Santiago blushed. "He's fine."

"If you see Officer Drake before I do, please thank him for me."

"Will do. See you later." Santiago left.

Vikki glanced through the list. The house numbers meant nothing to her. She'd visit the empty houses when people were there to find out if anything was amiss. Officer Drake hadn't mentioned anything about the homes that were occupied. She raised her head to see if Santiago was still around, she wasn't. But, the ME came stepped through the door.

CHAPTER EIGHT

"Hey, are you okay?" Ted said, approaching her desk. He checked his surroundings. Left, then right, acknowledging detectives with a nod here and a wave there as he approached Vikki's desk.

His blue scrubs peeked out under his unbuttoned white lab coat. Vikki couldn't tell if he'd gone home, showered, and returned. Or he'd freshened up and continued his work. One day blended into the next.

"Yes, it couldn't be better," Vikki said. A big smile parted her lips. "I spoke with Levin and told him about what we talked about last night.'

"What did he say?"

"He gave his blessing." Vikki glared at Gomez. "It's him who has reservations."

Ted smiled. "Gomez, what's your concern?"

Gomez raised both hands, palms out. "Don't get me wrong. I don't have a problem with it. It's just that sometimes you should let sleeping dogs sleep on. It happened long ago, and I doubt the NYPD didn't do a good job then. What do you think?"

Ted took a moment before he spoke. "No suspects were found. And the murders remain unsolved. Maybe it needs fresh eyes. Or new technology applied to the evidence gathered. Or prison confessions that need to be investigated."

Gomez scoffed. "Jailbirds are not trustworthy, but any new evidence is worth chasing down. Okay, I reverse my opposition. You can also count on me to lend a hand whenever you need me."

Ted raised both eyebrows. "Speaking of evidence, I recovered the bullet from Mary Beecham early in the morning. It was intact."

Vikki almost flew out of her chair. "We'll have to send it to ballistics right away."

"I'd already done that. I also put a rush on it."

"Thank you so much," Vikki said. She remembered what Mallory had said last night. Only a specially made bullet could penetrate glass, then the victim's skull, and remain intact.

Ted nodded. "I thought you should know so you guys can plan your day accordingly. I have to get back to the morgue. I have a road traffic accident victim to work on." He patted Vikki on the shoulder. "See you later." He headed for the door.

"You got me breakfast...thank you," Gomez said and reached for the croissant sandwich.

Vikki took a sip of her coffee and made a face. "I'll heat this in the break room. You want me to do yours, too?"

"I'll come with you."

They heated their coffee and food in the break room and ate there.

On their way back to the squad room, Vikki said, "What time do you think we should head back to the Coopers' to talk to the husband and the victim's father? Or should we invite them here?"

"Let's drop by. We might get a different perspective with daytime." Gomez shrugged. "We've eaten. We might as well leave now."

Vikki straightened her desk and reached for her jacket when her phone rang. "Mattsen."

"Detective Mattsen, this is the forensic lab," said a deep voice, all business.

Vikki's pulse picked up a notch. "Hello."

"We got a rush order early this morning from Dr. Brandon."

Vikki gripped the phone harder.

"I'm sorry, the signature on the bullet did not match any weapon in our database."

Vikki felt like a bathtub full of water and the plug suddenly removed. "Oh."

"But we found something unexpected. The striations matched those on another bullet recovered from a victim six weeks ago."

Vikki sat up. Hadn't Levin said it reminded him of another incident six weeks ago? She'd heard about the shooting while investigating the dead professor case. "What was the name of the victim?"

"One moment."

The sound of ruffling paper came from the other end of the phone. "It's Jack Jenkins. He was shot outside the St. Ives Mall. Similar to this case, he dropped dead on the spot. Nobody saw anything. I'll email the findings as an attachment."

Vikki thanked him and hung up. She turned to Gomez. "They found a match. Not the gun, but another bullet with the same signature as the one recovered from Mary Beecham. Another person was shot six weeks ago with the same gun."

Eyes alert, Gomez shook his mouse and woke up his PC.

"We'll need to retrieve the case file and talk to the detective handling it. What's the vic's name?"

"Jenkins, Jack Jenkins."

Gomez typed the name on his keyboard. "Peter Malone," he read from the screen. "He's on vacation." Gomez typed, hit enter, and read a little more. "There isn't much here. I'll print them out anyway." He clicked on the print and got up. "I'll go and get them."

Gomez headed for the printer tucked in the corner.

Vikki knew Peter Malone but hadn't worked with him one-on-one. He was an old-timer like Gomez. He had probably put in more time and was looking forward to retiring.

Gomez returned a few minutes later with the thinnest file Vikki had ever seen.

"There isn't much here." He handed the file to Vikki.

Vikki read quickly. When she'd finished, she let out a breath. "No suspects, no leads. Three eyewitness accounts are the same—the man was walking toward the entrance to the mall and dropped to the ground. No one remembered hearing a gunshot."

Gomez took the folder back from her and leafed through it. "It's like Malone couldn't make head nor tail of it, and now he's on vacation."

Vikki thought for a moment. "Let's go see Jack Jenkins' widow. We might learn something new."

CHAPTER NINE

Mrs. Jenkins lived on fifteen Bloom Road in St. Ives. A middle-class neighborhood with a row of one-story buildings with one car garages.

Vikki parked her white Ford Explorer on the road, and she and Gomez got out of the car. The garage door opened, and a red Toyota Camry slowly backed out of the garage. It came to a halt, and the garage door lumbered down.

A woman was in the driver's seat. She turned the car off and came out, her eyebrows drawn together.

"Mrs. Jenkins?" Vikki asked. She unclipped her badge and raised it. "I'm Detective Victoria Mattsen."

Mrs. Jenkins lifted her eyebrows. "Yes." She wore a camel coat, all buttoned up. Her shoulder-length brown hair was combed out. "The police? How can I help you?"

Vikki noted she spoke English with an Eastern European accent. "This is my colleague, Detective Mike Gomez. Sorry to bother you, Mrs. Jenkins, but we wanted to ask you a few questions about your late husband."

Mrs. Jenkins clenched her jaw and let out a breath.

"Where's Detective Malone? He hasn't called back since. Have you people caught the murderer?"

Vikki didn't know what to tell her. Not that he was on vacation, even though it was something he was entitled to.

"Mrs. Jenkins," Gomez said, stepping forward. "We're still working hard to find out who murdered your husband. All hands are on deck to find out what happened. There's a new angle we're focusing on, and we need your help. We have a few questions."

"I talked to your Detective Malone. I answered all his questions. Why not ask him?"

The cold was biting. Vikki looked toward the entrance to the house, hoping the woman would invite them in. "Does the name Mary Beecham mean anything to you?" Vikki watched the woman's eyes. She was relieved when she caught a flicker of recognition in them.

"I heard about the shooting this morning. It was in the local news. I can't believe this is happening in this community. You think it's related to my husband's case?"

"You think it's someone your husband could have known?" Gomez asked.

Mrs. Jenkins visibly shivered. "Mary Beecham...Mary Beecham. I can't remember him mentioning her. Maybe it was someone he knew, met on his own. I wouldn't know. It wasn't someone he worked with. I know those people. I've met some, and he talked about his coworkers. I don't remember hearing that name."

"We're trying to see if there was a connection between the two," said Gomez.

Mrs. Jenkins glanced at her car. "Ask Mr. Malone. He can help you. I answered all his questions, and there were a lot." She checked her phone. "I have to go. I have an appointment in the court. They want me to be on a jury. I want to see if I can be excused. Since registering to vote, the letters for jury duty started coming. I wish I hadn't. I don't like courts."

Vikki gave an encouraging smile. "It's your civic duty to vote and to serve on a jury."

Mrs. Jenkins narrowed her eyes. "Civic duty? That was what Jack said he was doing the last time I went to court. Civic duty."

"When was that?" Gomez asked.

"About three years ago. Jack was a witness." Mrs. Jenkins shook her head. "He and his dashboard camera. He said it was his civic duty to report what he saw." She glanced at her watch again. "I have to get going. There's nothing new I can add to your investigation."

"Sorry for keeping you waiting. But what did he see?" Vikki asked.

Mrs. Jenkins spoke through tight lips. "It was a road-rage incident. Jack loved his gadgets. He had a dashboard camera in case he got into an accident and determining who is innocent or guilty comes down to evidence. So he could say, here's the proof. I'm right, and the other driver was wrong."

Mrs. Jenkins paused at the sound of a car slowing down and driving past them. She stared into space as if reliving a similar discussion with her husband about why he bought the camera.

Mrs. Jenkins continued. "His camera caught three cars instead, two of them trying to run the third car off the road. Jack had no context of what was going on. His camera caught a flash of light, one of the two aggressor cars losing control and later slowing down." Mrs. Jenkins shuddered. That video convinced the jury and sent the driver of the one car to jail."

Vikki gave Gomez a questioning look only a partner could understand—if he'd heard about the crime.

Gomez shook his head. He turned to Mrs. Jenkins. "The driver of the car that was being bullied went to jail?"

Mrs. Jenkins nodded and took a step back. "I must go if I want to be excused from jury duty. I'm surprised you didn't hear about the case. A black man in Pennsylvania was with his girlfriend and toddler when a group of intoxicated teenagers pulled up beside his car and tried to run him off the road. He'd been dealing with their aggressive driving for about ten minutes before they passed Jack."

"Hold on. Mr. Jenkins was in Pennsylvania?" Gomez asked.

Mrs. Jenkin's hand was on the car door handle. "Yes, Jack was a traveling salesman. He sold insurance across the country. His camera caught the moment Malcolm West shot into one of the two cars. I must go now. Please give me your card. I'll call you if there's anything I remember."

Vikki fished out a card and gave it to her. "Please, just one more question. What did he go to jail for?"

CHAPTER TEN

Vikki drove toward the Cooper family home, her mind occupied with what Mrs. Jenkins had said. Involuntary manslaughter, she'd said. Malcolm West had said that DWB didn't help his stand your ground defense. DWB, Driving While Black, Vikki knew was the acronym used by people of color to explain what happened when they were stopped by police for no apparent reason.

Gomez said, "We didn't hear about the case, maybe because it took place in PA." He'd pulled up the case on his phone and read. "The jury didn't buy his stand your ground defense. Or in this case, defending his castle. Several juror members said the video made a compelling case for them. All they saw was Mr. West fire into the car without provocation."

"That's motive right there," Vikki said. "He comes out of jail and what's the first thing he does?" Vikki made air quotes with her hands. "Goes after the man who technically put him in there. Where's Malcolm West now?"

Gomez's thick fingers tapped on the keyboard. "Hold on." A moment later, he raised his head slowly and turned to

Vikki. "He's still in jail. He's been there for the past three and a half years."

CHAPTER ELEVEN

"I spoke to the police last night," Greg Beecham said. "I told them everything I saw."

With her notebook in hand, Vikki sat with Gomez and Mr. Beecham in his in-law's living room. Mr. Beecham wore the same jeans he had on yesterday but had changed his shirt. His eyes, red and puffy, like the embroidered pumpkin on his sweater.

"Do you remember the person you spoke with last night?" Vikki said. "Were they wearing a—"

Mr. Beecham cut her off. "I can't remember. Are you aware I lost my wife yesterday?" His voice had an edge to it. "We'd just finished dinner, and Mary collapsed on the floor with a bullet in her head. What are you doing about it instead of asking me questions of no value?"

Vikki considered bringing him to the station and thought the better of it. The man was grieving—everyone grieved differently.

"Mr. Beecham, I can't imagine what you're going through," Gomez said. "But our job is to find out who did this." He spoke in the best fatherly voice he could muster.

"Anything else you remember, even if you think it doesn't mean anything, might be the missing link and help complete the puzzle down the road."

Mr. Beecham pursed for a moment. "I'm sorry for my outburst. Not every day you see someone get shot, let alone your wife." He let out a breath through quivering lips. "Do you have any direct questions? I might do better with those?"

"Mr. Beecham—"

"Please, call me Greg."

Gomez gave a slight nod. "Greg, does the name Jack Jenkins mean anything to you?"

Greg pursed his lips and muttered the name several times. "Should it?"

"Six weeks ago," Gomez said, "Jack Jenkins was walking toward St. Ives Mall entrance when he was shot in the head. He died on the spot. Like your wife, he seemed to have been shot from afar. No one heard or saw anything."

Greg's eyes widened. "Jesus. Do you think my wife was involved in something that got her killed?"

"We don't know for sure. But the ballistics report on the bullet retrieved from your wife suggests it came from the same gun."

"You can figure that out just by looking at the bullet?" Greg asked.

Vikki nodded. "Like fingerprints, no two gun barrels are the same. They have different breech face marks, lands, and grooves on them, and the mark made by the firing pin as it struck the bullet. All these give the gun a particular signature, unique to it alone." She glanced at Greg. "The bullets recovered from your wife and Mr. Jenkins had identical marks."

For a moment, Greg's eyes were hopeful, then dimmed. "All that knowledge wouldn't bring her back."

"But it would help bring whoever gave themselves a God-like complex to justice," Gomez said.

"It's impossible for me to know everyone she knew. Mary couldn't have been involved in anything potentially harmful to her. She was afraid of her own shadow."

"Maybe it was something she saw without realizing," Vikki said. "Any recent travels for work or personal? Or interacting with new people?"

Greg stared into space. Like he hadn't heard her. "What could she be involved in that cost her her life? Maybe someone she met somewhere."

"Is there anyone you think would want to hurt your wife?" Vikki asked. "Someone who didn't like her?"

Greg rested his elbows on his knees and clasped his head in his hands. His little daughter skipped into the living room with Mrs. Cooper behind her. Mrs. Cooper had let them in when they'd rung the bell and took them to the living room where Greg was. Now she was back.

"Daddy."

Greg's face jerked up.

"Come on, Mary," Mrs. Cooper said. "Your daddy is having an important meeting with the detectives."

Mary ignored her and walked up to her father. "Daddy, when is Mommy coming home? She should be awake now."

Greg's lips quivered. He fought his emotions, but they won. "Come here." He hugged her tightly as tears rolled down his cheeks.

"I think he's had enough for one day," Mrs. Cooper said.

Vikki shut her notebook.

Gomez got to his feet. "We should be going now." He fished a card from his suit pocket and placed it on the coffee table. "Greg, we're so sorry for your loss. If you remember anything, please don't hesitate to call."

Mrs. Cooper took a step toward them.

Vikki pursed her lips and smiled at her. "Don't worry. We'll let ourselves out."

They headed for the exit.

Outside, they found Mr. Cooper sitting on the stairs. All he had on against the elements were a patterned flannel shirt, corduroy pants, boots, and a scarf around his neck.

"You'll catch a cold, sir," Gomez said.

The man shrugged. "Everything I have has been snatched from me. I'm empty inside." He raised his head. "I overheard what you asked Greg." He gave a slight nod. "I can think of someone wanting to hurt my little girl. I'd warned her to mind her own business, but she always wanted to do the right thing. That's the kind of person my Mary was. How can you argue with that?"

Vikki sat beside him on the stairs. Adrenaline rushed through her. "There was an incident?"

Mr. Cooper nodded.

"What happened?" Gomez asked.

"About two years ago, she testified against a coworker. Her testimony helped send him to jail."

Vikki's pulse changed gears once she'd heard the word testimony. She had questions but knew it was best not to interrupt someone providing information freely.

"In her job at System Inc.," Mr. Cooper said, "She worked in customer service during the first shift. One slow day, she played around with a password-protected folder on their hard drive. After several failed attempts, she typed in her coworker's initials, plus his last name spelled backward, and the folder gave up its secrets."

Vikki licked her lips and swallowed. She looked at Gomez, who was bright-eyed.

Mr. Cooper exhaled. "The folder was full of child porn. Images, videos—she reported it to the authorities of the company. They brought in the police, and soon her coworker lost his job and faced multiple counts of possessing child pornography. The police did their investigations, and the

District Attorney charged him. The case was a slam dunk for the prosecution."

Vikki's heart thudded. This was too good to be true. If this wasn't a clear case of motive, then she didn't know what motive was. This time she couldn't hold her mouth. "Do you know the name of the coworker who was imprisoned?"

"Peter Kay," Mr. Cooper said.

CHAPTER TWELVE

The drive back to the police station was lively. Now they had more names to deal with than before. Their first agreement was to get fast food.

Vikki drove into Burger King on their way to the police station around noon and stopped at the ordering terminal. The loudspeaker crackled, and the cashier asked for their orders. Vikki ordered two Whopper Juniors for herself and Coke, a Whopper with onion rings, and a Sprite for Gomez.

Gomez gave her a side-eye glance. "Who are the rings for?"

"I like fries, but my preference today, right now—is onion rings." Vikki paid, collected their food from the little window, and handed everything to Gomez.

He opened the paper bags, filling the car with the smell of fast food, and rummaged through. He exhaled when he found his sandwich.

Vikki's stomach rumbled at the smell. She didn't want to eat and drive, so she asked a question to keep her mind away from it. "You think the husband had any role in what happened to his wife?"

Gomez raised a finger and took a bite of his burger. He chewed, then swallowed. "That's where I was leaning before we saw her father on the stairs and he dropped a bomb."

Vikki chuckled. "That indeed was a bomb. I'm sure there must have been a lot of back and forth with her company's management before they decided to take the matter to the police. Cover your ass."

"C.Y.A!" Gomez said. "That's the first thing to think of before you make any move."

They were stuck in traffic for a while as they approached the exit that led to the mall. By the time they got to the station, Gomez's food was history.

Vikki parked the car and unwrapped her food. Gomez tried to forage into Vikki's onion rings, but she slapped his hands away.

"The whopper didn't hit the spot?"

Gomez laughed. He opened the door. "I'll leave you to eat in peace. I'll check the road-rage case and see what I can dig up. Take your time."

Through a mouthful, Vikki said, "Wait." She chewed and swallowed. "Let's not forget the husband. We have statistics on our side in the death of a partner."

"Okay, boss," Gomez said and stepped out of the car. "Who will do little errands like this for you after I retire? With the same amount of expertise?"

Vikki smiled. "Until we get there... Right now, it seems like a bridge too far."

Gomez tapped on the roof of the car. "See you inside."

Vikki finished her burger and worked on the rings. She wondered what motive Greg Beecham might have to murder his wife. Another relationship? Money? His alibi was solid. He was right there when it had happened. But he could have paid someone, guilty by proxy. But what could be his motive?

She finished her food, chased them down with Coke, and

made her way to the detective squad room. She didn't bump into anyone who engaged in more than small talk.

Gomez was at his desk. He'd taken his jacket off and rolled up his sleeves. "I checked the financial statements of the Beechams. Nothing out of the ordinary. No major deposits or withdrawals. Anything is possible, but I don't see Greg Beecham taking out a contract to murder his wife." He raised his hands and let them drop to his side. "Seeing him yesterday and today—the man is broken."

Vikki nodded. "Apart from Mary Beecham, we have a few more names to check out. Malcolm West, Jack Jenkins, and Peter Kay. I wonder if a single thread links them all together?"

"If we don't get anywhere with the rest of the names, we should try for a warrant for Greg Beacham's phone records," Gomez said. "And see if there's a smoking gun there. He's the only other person on the list who's alive." He picked up a document from his table. "Greg Beecham took out a million-dollar policy on himself. The wife didn't have one."

Vikki assumed a version of *The Thinker* sculptor with a finger on her chin. "Hmmm. Maybe the wrong Beecham was killed?"

Gomez stared at her for a few seconds. Growl-like laughter escaped his throat. "You didn't say that." He shook his head. "She pays someone to kill her husband so she could collect the insurance, or some other reason, and got killed instead. That will be the day."

The phone on Gomez's table rang.

"It must be Detective Sennet from PA. I called earlier and left a message." Gomez picked up the phone. "Hello, Gomez here."

"This is Bill Sennet, Detective. I'm returning your call."

Vikki leaned closer to Gomez. She almost perfectly heard

a deep, resonant voice from the other side of the conversation.

"In your message, you said you're interested in a case from a few years ago that involved Malcolm West."

"Thank you so much for returning my call," Gomez said. "Yes, I understand Mr. West is serving time for manslaughter."

"Yes, the Stand Your Ground or Castle Doctrine case. I remember it like it was yesterday. You have the right to protect and defend your home or vehicle from intruders and attackers without fear of prosecution. Mr. West claimed he did just that, protecting his wife and toddler from drunk teenagers trying to run him off the road. He was protecting his castle."

Gomez sighed. "But a jury of his peers didn't agree."

"Exactly. It polarized the community. The testimony of Jenkins and his dashcam video of the incident as it happened swayed some jury members. I understand Jenkins was murdered six weeks ago in New Jersey."

Gomez nodded and said, "That's why I'm calling. Yesterday, there was another murder, and the bullet retrieved from the victim had the same striations as the one used on Jenkins. A Mary Beecham. A California transplant from New Jersey. Does the name ring any bells?"

"Mary Beecham," Detective Sennet muttered. "I'm afraid not. "But similar striations indicate the same gun. Gangbangers?"

"On the contrary, highly sophisticated. The bullet was top-notch. Both victims were taken out with headshots, execution style. Nobody heard or saw anything. From your investigation of the case, were there any findings you think could connect to this?"

There was a pause. "Mr. West proclaimed his innocence throughout the trial," Detective Sennet said. "He claimed that the law failed him because he was a black man. A white man would have gotten a pat on the back and told to go his merry way—Mr. West's words. Would he go after the man whose testimony secured his defeat? It's possible. But the last time I checked, he was still in jail."

CHAPTER THIRTEEN

Gomez excused himself after talking to Detective Sennet and headed to the bathroom. Vikki pondered the phone call with the PA detective. The case had polarized the community and seemed to center around race.

Malcolm West claimed his rights as a law-abiding citizen when he'd been outnumbered and cornered. He'd protected himself and his family the best he could. Yet the law had failed him.

The man he'd said sealed his fate had been shot dead six weeks ago. Vikki wondered if the jurors themselves suffered the same fate as Mr. Jenkins. A light bulb went off in her head.

She Googled jury members in the trial of Malcolm West. The composition broke down as nine white jurors, two black, and one Hispanic. There were ten women and two men. Nine had graduated high school, one had no diploma, and two had college degrees.

Vikki cross-checked the names to a death records database. One white man and the lone Hispanic were dead. Her mouth went dry. She swallowed. Was this possible? Could this be related? On a piece of paper, she wrote the names Conrad Smith, thirty-one years old, and Jesus Aguilera, seventy.

Adrenaline rushed through her as she looked for the causes of death. Conrad Smith, she found first. Cause of death injuries from a road traffic accident. She typed Jesus Aguilera next. Cause of death—pneumonia. Vikki let out a breath. Neither was by a gunshot to the head.

She tapped her iPhone to wake it up. It was one p.m. Where was Gomez? They must come up with a plan.

To kill time, Vikki decided to call the Ashton Police Department in Long Island, New York. With trembling fingers, she thumbed in the query in the Google search bar and hit search.

"Ashton PD. Susan speaking, how can I help you?" The voice was female, neutral, and straight to the point.

"Hello, my name is Detective Victoria Mattsen. I'm calling about a homicide that happened twelve years ago."

"Ouch, that's a cold case. Do you have a case number or name of the victim?"

Vikki's heart was pounding. She was doing it. "Yes, names. They are Michael Devoe and Alexis Devoe."

"Can you spell the last name, please?"

Vikki did.

Susan said, "One second."

The breath rattled out of Vikki. This was the first step. She wondered if she should have taken Levin and Gomez's suggestion and let sleeping dogs lie. She shook her head. Who knows what would have become of her if it hadn't been for Alexis and her father? She probably would have been murdered.

"Detective?" Susan said.

"Yes."

"You'll have to make a formal request. Visit our website, and you'll see a tab for requests. Follow the prompts, and it will take you to a form. Complete the form, make the payment, and the documents will be sent to you, depending on your chosen option, email or hard copy."

Vikki was lost for words. "Couldn't we do it over the phone right now?"

"I'm sorry, we have a process and try to stick to it."

"Okay, will do."

Vikki hung up and went to their website. She filled out the form and made the payment. There was an option for both hard copy and snail mail. She chose both and hoped the digital version would come faster. That way, she'd start reading sooner rather than later.

She knew more about Malcolm West than yesterday, so the next port of call was Peter Kay. She typed his name into Google and wondered if Angie had covered the news when it had happened. She should call her.

Vikki hit search, and the dependable search engine returned several websites and digital blogs in Pike County, PA, with articles about him.

"Pennsylvania?" Vikki clicked on the first site.

An image of a middle-aged man, blond, with bloodshot eyes appeared above an article titled: *NJ Man, arrested for possessing child porn in a work computer.* She started to read, surprised that Mary Beecham had lived in New Jersey and worked in Pennsylvania.

The article was dated three years ago. Vikki had no sympathy for child molesters, preying on the innocent. She had her own scars. She pushed the thought away and began reading. Law enforcement picked Peter Kay up at his work-place after a tip-off by a coworker. They didn't mention Mary Beecham by name.

Vikki's cell phone rang. It was her friend, Angie Baxter. An investigative journalist for *The Chronicle*, she and Vikki had become fast friends when they'd first met a few years ago when Vikki had moved to St. Ives from New York.

Now and then, they walked a fine line to share information about ongoing cases without jeopardizing the investigations' integrity. Occasionally, Angie might have information that would help Vikki get a better grip on her case. Perfect timing.

"Hi, Angie, I was just about to call you."

"Of course you were," Angie said. She plunged straight into why she'd called. "Did I hear this right? Was a woman shot dead in her home after dinner last night? When were you going to tell me?"

"As I said, I was just about to call. The woman's name is Mary Beecham. She flew in from California with her husband and daughter to spend Thanksgiving with her parents. After eating dinner last night, she was shot dead."

"Vikki, I already have all that. I only needed you to confirm. What about the why and who?"

"That's where you come in. A St. Ives man working in PA was charged with child porn possession three years ago. He was convicted and is presently serving time in—"

Angie cut her off. "Monroe County Correctional Facility in Stroudsburg, PA. He said he was innocent, and the file was already on the PC. But when the police executed a warrant and searched his home, thousands of images and videos of children were found on several devices he owned. Despite his claims of innocence, a jury of his peers found him guilty."

Vikki nodded. But remembering Angie was on the phone, she said, "Good. Now the fun part. Six weeks ago, Jack Jenkins, a traveling salesman, was shot dead as he was about to enter the mall."

"Okay, I vaguely remember the case," Angie said. "What's the connection?"

Vikki had already told a lot to now hold anything back. "Remember, you can't print any of this."

"I already know that. Until you give the go-ahead, nothing is printed. You don't have to remind me."

Vikki continued. "The victim was also instrumental in convicting a man whose defense was the Castle Doctrine. He stood his ground and shot at the people threatening him, killing one of them. The bullet extracted from Jack Jenkins and Mary Beecham came from the same gun."

Angie was quiet for a moment. "So we can say that the same person shot both victims. Did the stand your ground guy also proclaim his innocence?"

"Yes."

"And both are still in jail, right?" Angie said.

"Mm-hmm."

"Then the answer to who's doing the shooting lies in jail."

CHAPTER FOURTEEN

Vikki finished the call with Angie with a promise to inform her once she uncovered anything new. She took a deep breath and let it out in a rush. She sank into her chair, eyes fixed on the monitor. Two good heads were always better than one. You never knew what you'd find, even the obvious right in your face.

Malcolm West and Peter Kay had solid alibis when the murder had occurred. They were in prison. Both proclaimed their innocence when the murders took place. Someone must have come across one or both in jail and heard their stories. The question was, where?

Vikki was oblivious to the sights and sounds around her until she noticed an approaching figure in her periphery and turned. Gomez was back. In his hand was a tray with two cups of coffee.

"Here," Gomez said. "Sorry, I couldn't help myself. I dashed out to get some coffee. I hope you didn't miss me too much."

Vikki took the cup. The smell of coffee cleared her mind. "Exactly what the doctor ordered." She shut her eyes and brought it to her lips, unsure whether it was black or flavored. She smiled. He'd got it right—French vanilla with a dash of sugar.

"From the look on your face. I didn't do badly on the coffee. Did you come up with anything new while I was away?"

Vikki put down her coffee. "I was researching Peter Kay and found out that Mary Beecham lived in St. Ives and worked about thirty minutes away in Pike County. Did you know that?"

"Pennsylvania?" Gomez shook his head.

"I spoke with Angie on the phone before you came back—"

"The girl reporter?"

Vikki nodded. "We talked about the two murders. She made it obvious that someone else was likely in the mix. Someone who met them and knew their stories. Either in the same jail or at different times. I know Malcolm West is in Monroe County Correctional Facility in Stroudsburg. I was about to search the database for where Peter Kay is doing time when you walked in." Vikki returned to her keyboard and accessed the USA correction database.

Gomez was nodding. "Since they're both in jail, they must have contracted someone to eliminate the people they blame for their incarceration."

Vikki hit enter and held her breath. The result came back fast. "My God, Peter Kay is also an inmate in Stroudsburg."

Gomez dragged his chair closer to Vikki's desk and sat. He stared at the screen with her. "It's likely they met the killer there." He cocked his head. "But how did they convince perp to murder on their behalf?"

Vikki threw out her hand. "Money. They paid him."

Gomez sat up, palms on each knee, sliding them back and

forth on his thigh. "I'm sure a hitman costs money. And both were not rolling in Do Re Mi."

Vikki tapped a finger on her lip. She checked the time at the top-right corner of her screen. It was one p.m. "Maybe we should visit them. Stroudsburg is about fifty-five minutes away. Maybe an hour and twenty minutes, give or take traffic and processing."

Gomez chuckled. "Mattsen, come on. No one waltzes into a prison to see an inmate without scheduling an appointment. You know that."

"Maybe the chief knows the warden or something. It's not a social call. We're trying to find a killer responsible for two murders we know of. There could be more. West or Kay must have run into this guy."

Gomez thought for a moment, then got up. "You're right. The only way to find out what's possible is to ask. Let's go see Levin."

"Both Malcolm West and Peter Kay are in the Monroe County Correctional Facility in Stroudsburg?" Captain Levin asked, glancing at Gomez and Vikki standing on the opposite side of the table.

They nodded.

Levin, dressed sharply in his navy-blue suit, exhaled. "There's no guarantee they'll talk, but it's worth a try. I know the warden, but we'll go with whatever time works for him. It's short notice." He leaned forward, flapping his hand for them to sit, and reached for the phone on his desk.

Vikki sat and scanned the office as if it was her first time here. Her eyes registered nothing, but her ears were primed, ready for the conversation about to start.

When the warden came to the phone, Levin sounded like he was planning a fishing trip with an old friend. They caught up on small talk, then Levin told him why he was calling. He gave him the names of the two men they were interested in. They talked some more, then Levin hung up.

"It's a go," Levin said. He glanced at his watch. "He said he'll have them ready for three in the afternoon. That gives you plenty of time. Sign out a vehicle if there's one available. The sooner this case is closed, the better for St. Ives."

"Thank you, sir," Vikki said and got up.

Levin spread out his hands. "What about New York? Any progress?" He tilted his neck. "I know people."

It took Vikki a second to figure out what he was talking about. "Oh, it's okay, sir. Don't worry about it. I'll take care of it. Thanks for offering."

"All right Neil," Gomez said. "We'll keep you posted."

Back at their desks, Vikki said, "Should we leave right away?"

Gomez consulted his watch. "One-thirty. One hour's drive should get us there by two-thirty—at least three. Let's go."

"Detective Mattsen," said a familiar voice behind her.

Vikki turned. Maria Santiago approached.

"Hi, Maria, what's up?" Vikki continued to arrange the folders on her desk.

"There's a man out front that came in to report a break-in, but nothing was—"

Vikki smiled. "Can you process it, please? We have to head to Pennsylvania."

"I think it's one of the houses from last night," Santiago said.

Vikki froze. "One of the ones where no one was home when the uniform checked?"

"Yes, the homeowner is still here. I put him in the confer-ence room. He said he caught the intruder on camera."

Vikki's eyebrows shut up. "What?"

CHAPTER FIFTEEN

Vikki marched toward the conference room with Gomez not far behind. She couldn't believe what she'd heard. The intruder had been caught on camera.

She turned to Maria. "And nothing was stolen?" That was a telltale sign of a break-in for a different purpose other than stealing.

"That's what he said," Santiago said. She opened the conference room door. Vikki and Gomez went through. She stepped in after them, shutting the door behind her.

Vikki smiled and extended her hand to the middle-aged, bald black man with a goatee. He was dressed in a black V-neck sweater and brown corduroy pants.

"I'm Detective Mattsen, my colleague Detective Mike Gomez." She pointed at Gomez. "You've already met Detective Santiago."

The man smiled, nodding. "I'm Dr. Martin, my wife, Princess. And that's my son, Ike."

He pointed at a sixth or seventh grader dressed in jeans and a blue sweatshirt. He waved shyly at them.

"Thanks for meeting with us," Dr. Martin said.

He spoke with the faint trace of an accent Vikki couldn't place. She smiled and said, "I understand you returned from vacation and realized your home had been broken into. Where did you return from?"

"Monaco, Monte Carlo. Nice," Dr. Martin said. "It wasn't exactly broken into. There was no sign of a break-in, only that my son realized that his book series was not arranged as he'd left it."

"At first, we thought he didn't know what he was saying," Princess said. "But then he got upset we weren't taking him seriously, and my husband took a look at the Ring camera video. He played it back and then saw it."

Vikki raised an eyebrow. "Saw what?"

Dr. Martin reached into his back pocket and brought out an iPhone. "Here, I'll show you."

"You have a video of the perp?" Gomez said, coming closer, doubt in his voice.

"Yep," said Dr. Martin. He pushed a button.

A man looking down, wearing a dark hoodie over a baseball cap, appeared close to the camera. He raised a gloved hand toward the camera, and the screen went dark. A second passed, and Gomez spoke up.

"Where's the burglar?" Gomez said.

"That was it," Dr. Martin said.

Vikki analyzed what she saw. The man wore gloves—no fingerprint from him touching the camera. She was missing something but couldn't place a finger on it. "Can you play it again, please?"

The doctor did.

"Gomez, did you see anything?" Vikki said.

"No, but we must get going if we want to see those guys in jail."

Vikki nodded. Gomez was right, but.... "Play it again if you don't mind, but at reduced speed."

Dr. Martin nodded. "Slow motion, sure."

The video replayed, this time slowly.

"Pause!" Vikki said. Her heart thudded. When the man raised his hand, his sleeve pulled back enough to show half a skull in a semi-circle.

"That's a tattoo," Gomez said.

"Wow, you're right," Dr. Martin said, looking again. "I didn't see that."

Vikki brought out her card. "Can you email that footage to the address on the card, please?"

"Sure." The doctor began downloading it to his phone and sending it to Vikki's email.

"The man covered the screen with something," Vikki said. "What did he use?"

Dr. Martin nodded. "Kids would egg your home when you're not there. I thought it was one of them playing a prank. It was chewing gum."

A tingle traveled down Vikki's spine—DNA. "Do you still have it?"

"Of course not. I tossed it in the trash," Dr. Martin said. "It was only when I met my neighbor at the grocery store, and he mentioned police activity last night and that someone was murdered, that I thought it might be related."

"Do you still have the trash?" Gomez said.

Dr. Martin nodded. "It's in the kitchen trash. It hasn't been emptied yet."

Princess's eyes were wide with terror. Her hand rested on her neck. "Do you think this has something to do with the murder?"

Vikki gave a noncommittal shrug. "I can't say for sure until we investigate, but it seems like the shooter used your son's room as a sniper nest."

"We'll have to get CSU over there quick," Gomez said. He tapped a finger on his watch. "Mattsen, we have to go."

Vikki nodded. She shook the doctor's hand and his wife's, too. "Thank you so much for bringing this in. We were on our way to Pennsylvania. Detective Santiago will take over from here."

"Please wait here," Santiago said to the family. "I'll be right back."

Outside the door, Vikki turned to Santiago. "Let Mallory know at once. Mention the chewing gum. They might still be able to recover DNA from it. We already have an appointment which the captain pulled some strings to make possible."

Vikki checked her email on her phone. The video from Dr. Martin was in her inbox. She forwarded a copy to James Madden, the resident computer geek in computer forensics, with a message to identify the tatts.

"We have to go," Gomez said. "We have traffic to contend with."

Vikki looked at the time on her phone. Her stomach all but dropped to her toes. "Oh, goodness. Let's go." She headed for the elevator.

CHAPTER SIXTEEN

Gomez drove the police department's plain black Ford Explorer with Vikki riding shotgun. According to the GPS, most of their driving to Stroudsburg would be on Route 80.

While Gomez drove, Vikki focused on identifying the tattoo on the intruder's wrist. She went on Google and searched for a circle with a skull. She didn't get any convincing returns.

She played the video repeatedly but didn't get any new insights. A little frustrated, she put the playback on the slowest speed.

"I hope Mallory and his investigator will be able to use the gum," Gomez said.

Vikki stared out the window and watched the parade of trees as they sped along. "If they find it, I think they should be able to extract DNA from it. I read in the *Smithsonian Magazine* that scientists extracted DNA from a five thousand, seven-hundred-year-old piece of Stone Age chewing gum unearthed in Denmark. The article said they reconstructed the ancient chewer's complete genome. Down to the prehistoric meal she ate and the microorganisms in her mouth."

"Get out of here. For real?"

Vikki shrugged. "I don't doubt them. I won't doubt who they match the DNA from the chewing gum to when they extract it." Her mind drifted to what a skull enclosed in a circle could signify.

"But I know Wrigley's wasn't around then," Gomez said. "What were they chewing?"

Vikki laughed. "Very funny. If I remember correctly, they said birch gum. Now don't ask me what that is." She glanced down at her phone. "Probably some secretion from the tree. We can always Google it."

They hit a traffic jam. Vikki's stomach muscles tightened. It was always a good excuse for being late, but lying didn't come easily to her anymore. There was nothing she could do. The Ford Explorer wasn't going to rise into the air and fly the rest of the way.

Vikki continued with the video. The sleeve had pulled back, and the skull and circle emerged. She noticed a light inner circle next to the thick one and a straight line that cut both circles at regular intervals. It was familiar. Then it dawned on her. "Crosshairs."

Gomez turned to face her. "What did you say?"

"The tattoo on the intruder's wrist is a skull caught in a crosshair."

"Like a sniper?" Gomez said.

"Yes. With the sophistication of his shots and bullet, our perp is most likely ex-military." Vikki exhaled. She felt like a balancing scale where the weights on both sides had been removed.

"Our perp is likely someone with a military background," Gomez said. "Calm and calculated and was in contact with West and Kay at one point or the other. That narrows down our focus."

"Right," Vikki said.

Gomez tapped on the screen of his phone on a platform on the dash. "I can see the facility. Our ETA is twenty minutes."

CHAPTER SEVENTEEN

Gomez pulled up in front of the prison.

The structure and building arrangements reminded Vikki of the high school in St. Ives they'd visited while investigating two murders. It was not lost on her the symbolism of the word "institution" in both places—an institution of learning on the one hand and a correctional institution on the other.

One glaring difference was the absence of luxury cars in the parking lot.

They were buzzed in, and Vikki entered one of the cleanest hallways she'd ever been in. It looked and felt like a hospital but without the odor of disinfectant.

The receptionist, a tall blonde probably in her late twenties, met them in the lobby. They exchanged pleasantries, and then she discreetly checked her watch.

Vikki expected her to admonish them for being late. Instead, she said, "Mr. Mittles is expecting you." She led them down the corridor, knocked on the second door on the right, and pushed it open.

A man with steel-gray hair wearing a tailored pinstripe suit stood. He had a million-dollar smile. What crossed

Vikki's mind was the warden in the movie *Shawshank Redemption*. He extended his hand.

"I'm Mr. Mittles, the warden. You must be Detective Mattsen." He shook Vikki's hand.

"Thank you for meeting us at such short notice, sir. We got delayed coming out, and the gridlock on Route 80 was something else."

"The important thing is you're here," Mr. Mittles said. "And you must be Mike Gomez. A veteran detective. It's a pleasure finally meeting you. I've heard a lot of good things about you from Neil." He shook hands with Gomez.

"The pleasure is all mine," Gomez said.

Mr. Mittles gestured to the two seats in front of his vast executive desk. "Please sit."

Vikki took in the office. A portrait of the warden and another of the state governor was on the wall behind him. A smaller version of the executive table with two monitors was also behind him. There was no chair, so he could slide back to use the computer if need be.

A bookshelf was placed against the wall. Plaques, plates, and glass memorabilia lined the top and different levels of the shelf. Next to it was an American flag—a patriot and a man who likes order, Vikki thought.

The warden sat ramrod straight. His palms made a steeple in front of him. "After talking with Chief Levin, I reviewed Mr. Malcolm West's and Peter Kay's files. They came in through different routes, manslaughter and child pornography possession. So far, they've been model inmates, and they both work in the laundry. Like everybody in here, they claim they are innocent."

Vikki's heart beat faster. So, the two men were in contact.

"So, how can we assist you?" said Mr. Mittles, his gaze bouncing from Vikki to Gomez.

Vikki pulled back, hoping Gomez had read Mr. Mittles as the type who would rather deal with a man.

"Thank you so much, Warden," Gomez said. "We're investigating a murder, and we think the blueprints were drawn here. We're searching for a man who interacted with West and Kay. Close enough to them that they shared with him the details of the court cases that got them here. Probably someone who worked with them and was released in the past four months."

The warden raised his head. "Kim, could you compile a list as Mr. Gomez requested."

Vikki looked over her shoulder, realizing the secretary had been standing there all along.

"Yes, sir," Kim said and left the room.

"You think your man will be on that list?" Mr. Mittles asked.

Vikki nodded. "We think he murdered Mrs. Beecham and Jack Jenkins because their testimonies were the deciding factors in putting West and Kay in jail. His motives we don't know."

The warden had a sly smile on his lips. "You developed a profile of this man?"

"From the evidence we've collected so far," Vikki said. "We know he's a sharpshooter. Well-trained, probably ex-military, and must have interacted with the two men over time to hear their story and decide for himself whether they were innocent of the crimes or railroaded in."

Mr. Mittles nodded. "That's interesting."

There was a single knock on the door, and Kim walked in. She handed a single sheet of paper to him.

Mr. Mittles took the paper and started to read. He chuckled and shook his head. His lips widened into a smile. "Alexander Morris, thirty-two. Worked in the laundry for twelve months. Worked closely with Malcolm West and Peter

Kay. Spent three years here for assault, and a graduate of The US Army Sniper School, Fort Benning, GA." He handed the paper to Gomez.

Vikki couldn't believe how close they'd come to the profile they'd created. She glanced at the sheet in Gomez's hand. A portrait of a non-smiling man with a square jaw and penetrating eyes, and a profile summary.

They could run with what they had, but Vikki hoped there was more. "Sir, thank you so much. I was wondering if anyone who had interacted with Alex Morris one-on-one, apart from the two inmates, could give us a summary of what he's like."

Mr. Mittles laughed. "We don't want to involve prisoners. I'd say one of the guards who covered the laundry room." He raised his head and nodded, and his secretary stepped out.

"What's your next step?" Mr. Mittles asked.

"We'll have to find Mr. Morris and bring him in," Gomez said.

Vikki nodded. She hoped CSU was able to recover the chewing gum. Now they had a name to compare it with. She turned to a sharp, hard knock on the door.

"Sir?" A young man stepped in. He was probably in his mid-twenties, wearing the blue uniform of a correctional officer.

The warden raised his hand and waved him closer. "Ah, Officer Godwin. Detective Mattsen and Gomez from SIPD in New Jersey. They have a few questions about Alex Morris."

Officer O'Brien's eyebrows shot up. "Sir, he was released two months ago."

Vikki smiled at him. "Yes, we know. We're interested in his relationship with Malcolm West and Peter Kay."

Officer O'Brien glanced at the warden. He gave him the go-ahead.

CHAPTER EIGHTEEN

"Alex was reserved," Officer O'Brien said. "He's soft-spoken, a man of a few words, and not as talkative as West and Kay. I'll say he was a good listener." The officer chuckled. "Like every other inmate here, West and Kay proclaimed their innocence. Morris, on the other hand, went against the norm. He'd say he was the only guilty person in Pennsylvania."

"Did he ever get into fights with other inmates?" Gomez asked.

O'Brien shook his head. "On the contrary, he's the guy who will turn the other cheek if there's an altercation than get in a fight. It's like he's always calculating the pros and cons."

Vikki wondered what he'd been in for. She could easily find out once she was back at her desk.

O'Brien continued. "In the time Alex Morris worked in the laundry, the only time I ever heard he was angry was when he got a letter from his wife."

Vikki did a double take. "Oh, he's married?"

"Yes," O'Brien said and smiled. He was clearly enjoying being the center of the action. "She'd written him to say she was leaving him to marry the guy he'd caught her in bed with."

That was news to Vikki. Her eyes darted to the warden, then back to O'Brien. "Was that the assault that got him jail time?"

"I should think so," O'Brien said. "I heard he came home early and caught her in bed with another man." He swallowed. "They say he accused the man of seducing his wife and turned him into minced meat. He didn't lay a finger on his wife. Then he gets a letter from her that she is divorcing him and going to marry the same bastard. Emm...his words, not mine. From then onward, he always talked of revenge."

"The fury of a man scorned," Gomez said, laughing.

Vikki smiled. The warden and O'Brien had blank stares.

An awkward silence followed.

"I guess that will be all," said Mr. Mittles and thanked the officer.

O'Brien was at the door when Vikki said, "Does Alex Morris have any tattoos?"

The officer stopped and turned. "On his wrist—a skull caught in crosshairs.

CHAPTER NINETEEN

After Officer O'Brien left the office.

The warden's gaze darted from Gomez to Vikki. "Who do you want to interview first, West or Kay?

Vikki didn't think it was necessary anymore. Based on what O'Brien had said and the confirmation of the tattoo, she believed they had their man. She gave a subtle head shake.

"We don't think it will be necessary anymore," Gomez said. "We believe we have our man. In fact, we should be heading back to sniff out his trail."

Mr. Mittles raised an eyebrow. "Oh." He stood. "In that case, I guess we're done." He shook hands with Gomez.

Vikki stood. "Thank you so much for all your help, sir." She shook hands with the warden.

By five p.m., they were on their way back to New Jersey. This time Vikki drove.

For some unknown reason, they could not log in to the SIPD network to do some work before they got to St. Ives, and rush hour traffic was at its peak.

"Shoot me now," Gomez said.

Vikki could relate. She took her eyes away from the

parking lot Route 80 had become to glance at Gomez. "We have to learn more about this Alex Morris guy."

"There's probably a murdered woman somewhere who nobody has discovered yet," Gomez said. "And, Alex Morris, long gone, too. My guess is he neutralized his wife or ex first. Helped his buddies out and is now in the wind."

Vikki pursed her lips. "But he's a sniper. The two killings he did were in public. Unless his wife lives in another town."

Gomez picked up his phone and tapped the screen with his finger repeatedly. "Finding out would have been a walk in the park if this thing connected. Maybe someone has a jammer in one of these cars and is messing with us. It didn't happen when we were coming."

Vikki laughed. "Maybe we didn't notice. We were talking about chewing gum. We know a lot more now than then. Who was chewing the gum." Vikki knew who might be able to help them. Traffic started to move as she reached for her phone on the dash. She speed-dialed Angie.

"Vikki! You found the shooter already?"

"Yes, something like that."

"Where?" Angie said.

"Stroudsburg."

"Stroudsburg? It sounds like a beer," Angie said. "Talk to me, Vikki. You didn't call me to play guess where I am at."

Vikki laughed. "You're on speaker. I'm driving with Gomez. We're—"

"Hi, Gomez," Angie said. "I feel your pain. Stuck in the car with a lunatic."

Gomez pointed at the phone and made a twisting motion with his finger around his temple. "Hello, Angie. I'm trying to keep sane. We can't connect to the internet."

Vikki continued. "As I was saying, we're stuck on Route 80 on our way back from Stroudsburg, Pennsylvania. We went to see the man Mrs. Beecham's testimony put behind bars. I need your help."

"This is interesting. Go ahead."

"We think our shooter's name is Alex Morris," Vikki said. "And his wife or ex-wife is a potential target or already deceased. Any news in neighboring towns about a dead woman shot in the head in public?"

"Wow," Angie said. "I just pulled him up. Ex-military. Tours in Iraq and Afghanistan. Works as a freelancer."

Vikki let out a breath. "Anything else?"

"Calm down. I'm scrolling and reading. Okay, I see it. War hero found guilty of assault. I'll read it out to you."

Angie read out exactly what they'd already learned from Stroudsburg.

"Angie, any mention of the wife's name?"

"Nope, I'll have to delve deeper. Let me call you back. Bye, Gomez."

Angie hung up before Vikki or Gomez could say goodbye.

Gomez sighed. "We're back to square one. I'll take a nap." He reclined his seat. "At least traffic is moving. I need to be wide awake when we get back. There's a lot to be done."

Vikki nodded. She kept her eyes on the road. They had a big to do list. On top of the list was finding either Alex or his wife.

CHAPTER TWENTY

Vikki sat at her desk staring at the monitor. It was seven-thirty p.m., and she was on her second cup of coffee. Staff from the day shift were mostly gone, replaced by those for the night shift.

Things hadn't been easy. She'd searched DMV records for Alexander Morris but got nothing. He probably didn't own a car.

Gomez had run his financials, and the last hit was from four years ago, the last time he'd used his credit cards before going to jail. It was like Alex Morris was still holed up, even though he'd served his time and had been released eight weeks ago. Vikki regretted turning down the opportunity to speak with Malcolm West and Peter Kay. Alex Morris's plans after incarceration must have been a major discussion between him and his friends.

Gomez walked into the squad room and flopped into his seat. "I asked dispatch to put out an APB with a description of Mr. Morris and a picture. Without a car to look out for, it's like trying to identify the geese that swallowed your key amongst a flock of them."

Vikki laughed. "Never heard that before." There was a pause. "I wish we'd stayed and interviewed West and Kay. We can't go back to Mittles and ask to see them."

Gomez exhaled. "Sure we can. But it won't be today. I'm not in a hurry to get back on that road."

Vikki lwt out a sigh of relief. Neither was she.

"Mattsen, Gomez. You're back from Pennsylvania?"

They both turned. The chief of SIPD's CSU, Dennis Mallory, stood at the entrance of the squad room. He approached them.

"Hello, Dennis," Gomez said. "I'm just curious, did your investigators find the gum in the trash? Mattsen here told me about scientists extracting DNA from five-thousand-year-old chewing gum."

"That was the least of our problems," Mallory said. "It was where they said it would be, in the kitchen garbage bin. We knew where to search for that one. Our challenge was combing through the five-thousand-square-foot home or focusing on the sniper nest, their son's bedroom. I heard you guys figured out the ink on the wrist and the perp."

"Yes," Vikki said and told him about Alex Morris and what they'd uncovered so far.

"Good job," Mallory said. "That narrows the net. It's a matter of time. I was on my way out and came in to say hello. Hopefully, I'll read he's been caught in the papers tomorrow."

The mention of paper reminded her of Angie. She picked up her desk phone and called.

"Hello, Baxter."

"It's me. We're back in the office. We're having a hard time finding any record of this man. It's like he came out of jail and vanished."

"He's not a ghost," Angie said. "What about the wife? She must know. Guys come out of jail, and the first thing they want is to get laid."

"I don't think they're still together," Vikki said. She remembered what O'Brien had said at the jail. The only time he'd gotten furious was when his wife had said she was getting remarried. Her pulse raced. "Angie, do you by any chance know his wife's name? Maybe from when he was arrested. I could check here but..." Vikki's voice trailed off. She was tired of searching.

"She must have been mentioned in the news article when he got arrested. Hold on."

The rapid *tap, tap, tap* of Angie's fingers on the keyboard filled the silence. Vikki gave Gomez a thumbs-up. Angie stopped typing, made some sounds, and then started again.

"I found a few things," Angie said. "Say you owe me."

"I owe you. What did you find?"

She got an uncontested divorce. I found that out by searching the public records database." She'd emphasized the word public. "And she reverted to her maiden name, she's now Denise Ross. Her fiancé, John Comack."

Vikki scribbled the names on a piece of paper on her desk. Wrote "database" and passed it to Gomez.

"She put a wedding announcement in *The Chronicle*," Angie said. "And her wedding date was the twenty-third of September, roughly eight weeks ago."

"That would have been about when he was released from jail," Vikki said in a low voice. If they found Denise Ross, they'd find Alex Morris. Her stomach tightened. Denise Ross could already be dead.

"Are you still there?"

"Yes. Thanks, Angie. I have to go. Locating Denise Ross holds the key to finding Alex Morris. I'll call you." She hung up.

"I've pulled up the names," Gomez said. "John Comack is thirty-two, a computer engineer, and lives at seventeen Fox Run in Beckham Township."

Vikki knew Beckham Township. She'd worked with the sheriff on a case once. She was dependable.

"Denise Ross is twenty-eight, drives a Ford Focus, and lives in Beckham Township. Same address as Comack, but works as a manager at StoreShop, a grocery store in St. Ives."

"Let's go over to StoreShop," Vikki said. "It's closer, and if she's not there, they might know where she'd be, rather than meeting an empty house."

"I'm on the fence about putting out a BOLO for her," Gomez said. "What do you think?"

"Let's hold off on that for now. We don't want to create a tense situation. Uniforms are already busy with Thanksgiving shopping and madness for now. We'll play it by ear."

Vikki grabbed her peacoat from the back of her chair. She hoped they were not too late.

CHAPTER TWENTY-ONE

The glass door to the grocery store slid back as Vikki approached. Gomez was not far behind. Shoppers pushing carts or carrying baskets walked up and down the aisles. Hidden overhead speakers spilled out "Jingle Bells."

"Christmas songs already?" Gomez muttered. "They couldn't wait for Thanksgiving to be over first."

"What do you want them to play?" She stopped and scanned the store while waiting for Gomez to reply. "Do you know any Thanksgiving songs?"

It was a beehive of activity. Apple cider fragrance hung in the air like drying paint. Pumpkins and orange-colored Thanksgiving-theme decorations were strategically placed all over the store. She shopped here sometimes and wondered if she'd ever interacted with Denise Ross.

Gomez waved a dismissive hand. "Let's go toward their break room. There's always store staff going in or coming out of that area."

They'd entered through the fruit and vegetable entrance, and shoppers there had mostly fruits and vegetables in their carts and baskets.

A tired-looking, petite blonde woman wearing the store's apron walked briskly toward them. Her face focused ahead as if she were on a mission. On her apron was a tag that said Bella, next to a yellow smiley face button.

"Excuse me," Vikki said.

The woman raised her hand. "One moment." She pointed behind her. "I'm helping another customer. I'll be with you soon."

She continued without breaking stride. Behind her, a woman pushed a cart after her.

"I'll check out the break room," Gomez said. "There might be someone to talk to." He jerked his head toward the woman disappearing behind a refrigerated display of peeled fruits in containers. "Keep close to her. I think she'll give you her full attention once she finishes with the woman she's with."

Vikki nodded. "That makes sense. I think she's a manager, too."

Gomez continued toward the door that led to the break room. Vikki headed for the fruit section. She found Bella at the opposite end from where she stood and headed in her direction.

Bella pointed out some products on the shelf to the woman.

The woman smiled, and Vikki saw she mouthed the word "thank you." Bella turned and headed toward Vikki with a frown on her face. Recognizing Vikki, her scowl transformed into a grin. Vikki smiled.

"Busy night?" Vikki said when she got within earshot.

Bella pursed her lips and rolled her eyes. "Tell me about it." Her smile returned. "I was coming back to see if you still needed me. How can I help you?"

"Is Denise Ross working tonight?"

The smile on Bella's face faltered. "Why...why do you want to know?"

Vikki was taken aback. She started to unbutton her jacket. "I'm Detective Mattsen. I'm with SIPD." She opened the last button, unclipped her badge, and showed it to her.

Bella pursed her lip and nodded, the worry lines on her face deepening. "How can I help you?"

Vikki took a breath. She had to word this carefully. She didn't want to cause unnecessary panic. "We're investigating a case, and her name came up. We'd like to talk to her."

Bella's eyes widened. "We? Is she okay?"

"I'm here with my partner. We split up to find someone to talk to. Did something happen?"

Bella let out a long exhale that dragged her shoulders down. "Come, let's talk in my office. I'm Bella, the night manager."

They headed in the direction where Gomez had gone. He raised his eyebrows as they approached. Vikki introduced them.

"Come with me," Bella said. She led the way down a short corridor, past a bulletin board to a door with Floor Manager written on it and opened it.

It was a typical office space in a store. A hard plastic-top desk with several metal plastic chairs. Shelves filled to overflowing with files and documents. Bella didn't bother to sit. She started talking.

"I'm afraid for Dee...Denise. I heard her husband, her ex, is out."

"Did he come looking for her?" Vikki asked. Her voice was forceful.

Bella's eyes widened. "No...I-I don't think so."

"We're trying to find him and thought maybe he'd dropped by," Gomez said.

Bella let out an exaggerated laugh. "Dropped by? That's the last thing Denise wants."

"Why's that?" Gomez asked, feigning ignorance.

Bella pinched her lips, turned away, and gave a subtle shake of her head.

"Ma'am," Gomez said. "If there's anything you know, please tell us. Time is of the essence."

Bella exhaled. "Dee...Denise and I have been friends for a long time. She used to be married to Alex. He was in the military and never around. After he got discharged, he became a private contractor and was still never home for her, traveling to different hot spots all over the world."

"Private contractor," Gomez said. "Gun for hire. Marriage is already tough even when the couple is together."

Bella nodded. "She...she, Denise, met someone else." Bella's voice was low. She inhaled and let it out in a rush through her mouth. "One day, Alex returned unannounced and walked in on them."

Vikki knew where the story was going, but she wanted to hear someone else describe what had happened.

Bella took a deep breath, exhaled, and continued. "Denise said Alex was calm until John found his voice and said he was in love. Denise described Alex's reaction as green light jumping to red without the yellow in between. Alex became a monster and brutalized John, accusing him of seducing his innocent wife. After that, he called the police."

Gomez raised an eyebrow. "Wait, Mr. Morris called the police himself?"

Bella nodded. "He got four years for assault."

"Listen to me carefully," Vikki said. "Alex Morris was released from jail eight weeks ago. It seems like he disappeared, but there was a murder last night which we think he was involved with. We believe your friend is in danger."

Bella placed her palm on her chest. "Oh my God."

"Where is Denise Ross now?"

"After their wedding on the twenty-third of September, they embarked on an eight-week vacation to travel the world," Bella said. "She hoped her job would be here when she got back. She's an asset here. We kept it for her. John is IT and can work from anywhere. She's scheduled to return tomorrow."

Vikki exhaled. She shot a glance at Gomez. "Maybe that's why he decided to help out West and Kay. He didn't have access to her."

Gomez stood up straight, rubbed his hands together, and blew out a huge breath. "Denise needs protection as we try to locate Mr. Morris. Do you have her itinerary? When is her flight coming in?"

Bella shook her head. "You misunderstand me. Denise came back this morning. She's returning to work tomorrow."

Vikki's pulse picked up a notch. "Who knows she's coming to work tomorrow?"

Bella raised her hand in a helpless gesture. "Everybody." Her gaze shifted.

Vikki's eyes followed. A big 'Welcome Back Denise!' sign was pinned on the bulletin board. It even listed Denise's favorite Chinese restaurant that will be catering the food.

"We have to assume Alex Morris has that information too," Gomez said.

Vikki's stomach tightened. She was already moving. She stopped at the door. "Do you have her phone number?"

"Yes, but she turned it off after she called me."

"We have to get to her home in Beckham Township."

CHAPTER TWENTY-TWO

John Comack's address was in a high-brow apartment complex. The type that catered to Manhattan moneybags who didn't mind the one hour commute to the city for work and live in a community where their money went far.

Vikki pressed her badge against the glass door and rapped on the surface with the other. It was inky-dark out, but the walkway to the entrance was well-lit.

A uniformed receptionist approached; his eyes focused on her badge. He pulled the door open. He stepped aside, forehead furrowed, eyebrows drawn together. "Good evening, how can I help you?"

Vikki reclipped her badge and stepped in. "I'm Detective Mattsen, and this my partner, Detective Gomez. What's Mr. Comack's apartment number and floor?"

A slow smile returned to the receptionist's face. "Oh, he's in two hundred and four, second floor. He came back this morning from a two-month honeymoon." He grinned. "He ordered a lot of food. The delivery girl went up not too long ago. Is he having a party? He didn't notify us."

Gomez scanned the reception area. "Where's the elevator?"

The receptionist pointed.

"Ah, thank you," Vikki said. She'd been searching for it too. "It blended with the wood-paneled walls."

"We'll ask him when we see him," Gomez said.

Vikki hit the number two button, then inhaled and exhaled. "You think they're having a party? It's late." She brought out her phone and shook it awake. The time was nine-fifteen p.m. "Maybe they don't want to cook yet and ordered a lot of food for the week."

The elevator door dinged and slid open. An arrow on the wall opposite indicated two hundred and four was on the left. They arrived at the door. Vikki knocked.

She waited a few moments and knocked again. All they got was dead silence. "You think it's soundproof?"

Gomez raised a finger and cocked his head.

Vikki listened.

"No! No! No!" It was a woman's voice. And it was filled with terror.

Was Alex Morris there already? "Mr. Comack! This is the police! Open the door!"

Images of what could be happening flashed through Vikki's mind. She pounded the door with her fist.

"Mattsen, out of the way."

She looked over her shoulder, then moved to the side. Gomez had stepped back. He raised his leg and aimed a kick above the door's handle.

Nothing happened.

Vikki's Glock was in her hand.

Gomez hit the door a second time. It flew open, followed by the bark of a gun.

CHAPTER TWENTY-THREE

The smell of Chinese food, the sharp tang of gunpowder, and blood hit Vikki's nostrils all at once. Her heart sounded like a jackhammer ripping up concrete. Her ears buzzed from the sound of the gun.

A woman in a blue sweater and jeans lay on her back on the bed, eyes wide open with a hole in the center of her forehead. A fast-spreading halo of blood surrounded her head. Vikki didn't need to feel her pulse to know she was dead.

A man in his underwear was tied to a chair. Tears streamed down his face. He whimpered something unintelligible. Vikki ignored him for now, her focus on the woman with a gun.

Vikki held her weapon in a double grip, the nozzle pointed at the tall woman wearing a long black winter coat and holding a long rifle. "Drop the gun!"

The woman, her back to Vikki, held the rifle by the forestock, arms stretched out. She bent her knees slowly and placed the rifle on the floor.

"On your knees! Interlace your fingers behind your head!"

The woman did so.

Gomez was in her periphery, his gun also covered the woman.

Vikki holstered her Glock and grabbed her handcuffs from her belt. She cuffed the woman with her hands behind her back. She did not resist.

Gomez called it in. "One civilian down! Send an ambulance and backup now!" He rattled off the address.

"He killed her," the man tied to the chair muttered.

Vikki paused and walked in front of the woman kneeling on the floor. Her hair was at an odd strange angle. Was she wearing a wig? There was a strong resemblance to the image of Alex Morris she'd seen earlier. "Mr. Morris?" Vikki reached for her gun. With her free hand, she yanked at the woman's hair. It was a wig.

The man laughed. "Yes. I'm Alex, Alex Morris." He turned toward the man whimpering. "Hey, John, how does it feel to have something you love taken away from you?"

John Comack let out a blood-curdling wail.

Alex nodded. "Now you can feel my pain. I've been planning this for years. That was what kept me going. You came with your honey-coated cock, seduced her, and took away the only person I ever loved."

Vikki knew they had to advise him before he said more to implicate himself. Or they might have a compromised case if it got debated in court. She couldn't help herself. She turned on the cellphone's recording app. But Gomez came to the rescue.

"Mr. Morris, you are under arrest for the murder of Mary Beecham and Denise Ross!" Gomez said. "You have the right to remain silent. Anything you say can and will be used against you in a court of law."

Mr. Morris remained quiet until Gomez was done with the Miranda rights.

"I knew she'd drop her guard once I didn't contest the

divorce," Alex said. He turned to John Comack. "I have a riddle for you. What type of honeymoon takes eight weeks?

A gut-wrenching sob escaped Comack's lips.

"Wrong answer," Mr. Morris said. "The one that ends with your bride getting shot in the head." He tossed his head back and laughed.

He must have lost his mind, Vikki thought.

"They say an idle mind is the Devil's workshop. While I waited for you to return, it gave me time to help my buddies out."

"What do you mean, help your buddies?" Vikki asked. "Did Malcolm West and Peter Kay plan this with you? Did they ask you to eliminate Mary Beecham and Jack Jenkins?"

"No, it's all me. Those two are pussies. Got thrown into jail for crimes they didn't commit. People bore false witness against them, and they paid dearly for it. I was the only guilty one among the three of us. I did the crime, and they did the time."

The elevator dinged. More voices and footsteps reached them, and footsteps filled the air and got closer and closer.

Vikki told the first uniform who came in that Alex Morris was under arrest for murder and should be taken into custody.

Medics descended on John Comack. They untied him and asked him if he was wounded or on any medication. A stretcher was brought up, and soon he was whisked away.

CHAPTER TWENTY-FOUR

Vikki and Ted had a quiet evening, just the two of them. Vikki sent her regrets to Gomez and Levin. Thanksgiving was a family affair, and she and Ted were gradually getting there.

Vikki ordered everything they needed from the grocery store where Denise Ross had worked.

"Alex Morris is going away for a long time," Ted said. "He loved his ex-wife so much he didn't want to hurt her the first time he found out she was cheating on him."

Vikki shrugged. "He must have changed his mind in prison." She sighed. "Divorce is always an option. I wonder why neither of them took that path until it was too late. Some marriages are like a boat in rough seas, rising and falling with the tide. And when it's obvious there's irreparable damage, and the boat is going down, instead of escaping in the lifeboat, some folks hang on tight and go down with the boat." She eyed Ted and wondered if they'd get to a stage where they couldn't stand each other.

Ted chuckled. "How do you know so much about marriage? Have you ever been married?"

She looked at him for a beat. "Nope. Same way as the

Catholic priest that councils on marriage. He's never been married."

Ted smiled, shaking his head. His face became serious, and he raised his wine glass. "To friendship, love, and finding out what happened to Alexis and Mike in the New Year."

The end.

ABOUT THE AUTHOR

Ifeanyi Esimai is a mystery and crime writer and enjoys reading across different genres. When he's not writing or reading, he's exploring documentaries on museums and ancient history.

Click here or the image to get all ten books!

Get a FREE copy of The Rookie!

Join my reader group for updates, giveaways, teasers, and a FREE copy of the prequel - The Rookie. Click here or scan the QR code

Prologue

Mindy watched snowflakes float like feathers through fogged windows. She was dressed for rolling around in the snow, and the blast from the car's heater made her feel like she was trapped in a sauna.

She glanced at her six-year-old brother playing a hand-held game wearing a puffy red jacket. Underneath it, she knew, he was a sweater and tee shirt like hers. He had a red scarf around his neck. He must be toasty in there.

Mindy's outfit was similar but a different color. Her jacket was pink with abstract designs of Christmas trees, snowflakes, and Santa. A purple beanie with a single white pompon perched on her head of shoulder-length blonde hair. She had on blue jeans and snow boots.

They were dressed warm enough to walk to the North Pole to see Santa. She'd be this miserable if Lisa, their nanny, had taken them to see Santa in the mall. Now she'd left them in the parking lot, in a sauna of a car, and dashed into the mini mall, with an 'I'll be back' spoken over her shoulder as she'd run off.

The air in the car smelled of burned plastic and sweat—like her school changing room after PE. Mindy glanced at the dashboard and wished she knew which button to push to turn down the heat and its noise.

Lisa had left the radio on to keep them company. Nat King Cole's "Merry Christmas to You" blasted from the speakers. This was the last straw. Their parents must know about this once they returned from their trip today. She'd tell them herself. Lisa would be fired.

She'd tell them about Lisa's boyfriend. He'd drop in once her parents left, and they'd be making kissing sounds in the guest bedroom. And worst of all, she didn't let them see Santa at the mall and left them in the car for hours while she went off on her own.

Mindy knew which of her parents to tell. Not her dad. He'd laugh and say he'd talk to her and never would. But Mommy—she'd call the cops on her.

Mindy knew all about the anti-child lock. There was no getting out of the car from the back. She climbed over to the front passenger seat.

"What are you doing?" Andy asked, focusing on her face, his Nintendo Switch held up in front of his face.

"I'm getting out of the car before we roast in here. You can come if you want. We can go to the pond and skate."

Andy leaned forward, his eyes wide. "We'll get in trouble with Lisa. And she'll tell Mom and Dad."

Mindy was two years older than her brother and sometimes pushed him around. "Don't be a crybaby. She won't tell. She left us in the car on our own. We can always say it was too hot, and we got out. But we'll be back before she comes out. We're only going to skate." She opened the front passenger side door and stepped out.

Cold air slammed into Mindy. It took a few seconds to go from uncomfortable warm to okay cool. She opened the back door for Andy. "Grab the skates."

"Mimi, are you sure?"

"Do you want to skate or not?" Mindy asked.

Andy grumbled. "All right." He dropped his Switch, picked up his skates, and exited the car.

Mindy rolled her eyes. "You should have brought mine, too." She leaned in and took her skates from the backseat.

She led the way, snow crunching under their feet.

The pond was in a small playground close to the mini mall. They'd been there a hundred times. She shot a look at the white Honda Accord. It was sandwiched between two cars in the parking lot, and their footprints were on the freshly fallen snow. Lisa had breadcrumbs to follow to find them whenever she came out.

Nobody was in the playground. The slides, swings, and monkey bars all had snow on them. Mindy sat on the snow and tried to take off her snow boots. With her mittens on, it wasn't working. She took them off and got a better grip.

Andy was struggling with his boots, so she helped him.

She took off her boot and slipped on her skates. By the time she was done, her fingers were hurting from the cold.

Andy walked with slow strides to the frozen pond. He was a good skater.

Mindy had planned to get on the ice first to ensure it was hard enough, but her brother was too eager.

"Andy...wait."

He stepped on the ice, smiled, and took off toward a bush in the pond.

Mindy examined the surface—frozen, with a dusting of snow. She could tell other kids had skated earlier from the blade marks on the ice. She smiled, safe enough. Now, it was their turn.

"Mimi!"

Mindy's head jerked up. "An-Andy?" Her heartbeat sounded like drums. "Andy!" She skated toward the bush. Did he fall in? Now she'd be dead for sure. Their parents wouldn't spare the rod if anything happened to Andy.

Mindy let out a sigh of relief. Andy was gazing down at something.

"Mimi! I-I think Santa is under the ice."

"What?" Mindy came closer. A big red object was partially covered with ice and snow. A bearded white face with blue eyes stared at her.

"Mimi, I think Santa fell off his sleigh and landed in the pond. Now he's frozen."

Mindy had only seen a dead body on TV. A scream ripped through her lips.

Chapter 1

Vikki and Ted met for a quiet, late lunch at Ziti Plus, a restaurant in Milton. Away from St. Ives for some privacy. In the background, an instrumental version of "Jingle Bells" provided a musical backdrop, mingling with chatter, mirthful laughter, and the clattering of utensils on plates from patrons already immersed in the holiday spirit.

The receptionist ushered them to a table. "And what drink should I get you?" The question was directed at Vikki.

They both ordered water since they were still on the job. Vikki's entree was chopped mixed salad and grilled chicken in a balsamic sauce. Ted ordered a well-done Angus beef burger served with seasoned fries.

Vikki rearranged the hem of her cream turtleneck sweater over her black pants. She preferred that her Glock 19 remain out of sight. Her Carmel jacket was draped over the back of her chair, her gloves and hat in the pocket. On her feet were ankle leather boots with rubber soles. Vikki was ready for whatever the weather had to bring.

Ted had on a long-sleeved tee shirt under his scrubs. He unzipped his puffer jacket but did not take it off.

Their food came, and they dug in.

Outside, it had stopped snowing. It wasn't enough accumulation to clog the roads with snowplows. There was already snow on the ground, and the new snow added a fresh dusting of white on cars, trees, and houses, enhancing the white Christmas ambiance.

The waiter removed their plates and dropped off their dessert. Velvet cake for Vikki, coffee for Ted. Once she left, Vikki leaned forward in her chair.

"What should we do for Christmas?"

Ted took his time adding a teaspoon of sugar and stirring the coffee.

Vikki cocked her head. "Is it a hard question?"

Ted chuckled. He had a glint in his eyes and ran his palm over his clean-shaven head. "I was thinking of getting a train set and you helping me put it together over the holiday." He stroked his goatee. "Then watch a Christmas movie marathon on TV and participate in any other marathon two people can do together."

Vikki batted her eyelids. "Like a two-person marathon? Elite runners finish in two hours. Do you have the stamina?"

"I'll do better. I'll finish in four—more time…[Click here to continue]

www.ingramcontent.com/pod-product-compliance
Lightning Source LLC
Chambersburg PA
CBHW070912100726
47907CB00008B/2299